The Rake
with
Cousin Winifred

❦

Amy Watson

© Amy Watson 2012

The moral right of the author has been asserted

No part of this publication may be reproduced, stored in a retrieval system, or transmitted in any form or by any means without the prior permission in writing of the publisher. Nor be otherwise circulated in any form of binding or cover other than that in which it is published and without a similar condition including this condition being imposed on the subsequent purchaser.

This book is a work of fiction. The characters and incidents are either fictitious or are used fictitiously. Any resemblance to any real person or incident is entirely coincidental and not intended by the author.

Table of Contents

The Rake 1
Cousin Winifred 211

The Rake

Chapter One

'Wish me luck,' said Alexander.

Miss Elizabeth Carstairs stood on tiptoe and kissed her childhood friend Alexander Masterson, better known as Sandy, on the cheek. 'You won't need luck, Arabella will be a fool if she doesn't fall in love with you.'

He pulled a rueful expression. 'I'll settle for her dancing with me, at least to begin with. It will be more difficult to get her to fall in love with me.'

'No it won't. You're young and you're handsome, and on top of everything else you're an earl. What more could any young lady want?'

'I don't know, that's what I keep asking myself,' he said, with a bewildered air.

'You just haven't met the right young lady,' Lizzie reassured him. Sandy was adorable, but he often seemed three years younger than her instead of three years older. 'When you do, you'll marry and settle down and I'll do the same, and we'll live near each other and take our children fishing together, as we always planned.'

'Before I can have children I have to find a wife,' Sandy reminded her.

'You're already besotted with Miss Arabella Wentworth,' said Lizzie, 'it's a start. Now go on, or else you're going to be late, and so am I. I'm going to Lady Farnby's rout this evening and I haven't even started to get dressed.'

Sandy picked up his tall hat and walked out of the

room.

He isn't bad looking, thought Lizzie as she watched him go, in fact he's quite handsome, in a funny kind of way, but I don't think Arabella will fall in love with him. She's very particular and of course she can have her choice of men.

The clock chimed, reminding her that she was late. Luckily Lady Farnby lived in Upper Grosvenor Street, which was practically round the corner, so it shouldn't take her too long to get there.

She called her maid and then went up to her bedroom. It was a pretty room at the back of the house with sprigged curtains, a carved fireplace, a four poster bed and a merry fire - which was a good thing because it was February and it was very cold.

Lizzie gave a sigh of relief when she saw that her ball gown had already been laid out on the bed. She took off her day dress and washed in the water Milly had carried up the stairs, then she slipped into her chemise and drawers before Milly fastened her stays and helped her into her dress. It was made of sky blue crape and it had a high waist, puffed sleeves and lots of frills round the bottom. She thought it was adorable and she hoped Jane and Sophy would like it, too.

She struggled to sit still whilst Milly put her feathered head-dress in her hair then she hurried downstairs.

'There you are at last!' said her mother, an elegant woman dressed in a stylish satin gown.

'Sandy -'

'I should have guessed,' sighed her mother. 'Whenever you're late it's always something to do with Sandy. Next time he calls make sure you send him away as soon as it's time to get dressed.'

'He wanted me to wish him luck. I couldn't just bundle him out the door, he needed reassuring.'

'Alexander always needs reassuring,' said her mother with a snort.

The carriage pulled away from the kerb and rumbled away down the streets.

Lizzie decided it was better not to say any more. Her mother had never understood Sandy. It wasn't that there was anything wrong with him, it was just that he was nervous with people he didn't know, and he needed plenty of encouragement.

She quickly forgot Sandy's problems when the carriage pulled up outside Lady Farnby's house. As she was shown into the drawing-room she found that Sophy and Jane were already there. She made straight for them, saying how pretty Sophy's pink satin ballgown was and how much she liked Jane's yellow silk dress.

'I'm so glad Madame DuPris managed to finish it on time,' said Lizzie, as Jane gave her a twirl. Jane had been worried that it would not be ready.

'So am I,' said Jane. 'She brought it over this afternoon, just in time.'

'Your dress is lovely, Lizzie,' said Sophy. 'It makes your eyes look blue.'

'Does it really?' Lizzie asked, pleased.

Jane and Sophy nodded encouragingly. Lizzie's eyes were really rather grey, but it was much nicer to think they were blue.

'Have you seen Sandy?' asked Jane. 'I thought he would be here tonight, but I haven't seen him yet, which is funny because I know he's in town.'

'Yes, he is,' said Lizzie. 'But he's not here. He's gone to Lady Hansdowne's ball instead.'

'What would he want to go there for? Lady Hansdowne's balls are ever so dull,' said Sophy.

Lizzie said, 'Arabella.'

'Arabella Wentworth?' asked Jane.

Lizzie nodded.

The three girls looked at each other and pulled a face.

'I don't know what the men all see in Arabella,' Sophy said.

'Golden hair,' suggested Lizzie.

'Azure blue eyes,' offered Jane.

'Oh, well, there is that,' said Sophy. 'But she's terribly spoilt. I can't think why the gentlemen don't see it.'

'Because they're too busy looking at her white bosom,' said Jane matter-of-factly.

All three girls were silent. Arabella's white bosom always looked wonderful. Even though there was never any more of it showing than was decent it drew the eye. And if it did that to the female of the species, what must it do to the male?

'I can never keep my face and arms white, no matter what,' sighed Sophy. 'The only way to do it is to stay indoors all summer, or wrap myself up in yards of muslin whenever I go out, as well as remembering to wear my gloves and my hat.'

'I tried it once,' said Lizzie. 'Sandy couldn't stop laughing.'

'It's funny how different he is with us,' said Sophy. 'He's not tongue-tied, I mean, he's always fun to be with, but when he's with people he doesn't know . . .'

'That's just the trouble,' said Jane. 'He's all right with us because he knows us, so he doesn't need to be nervous because he doesn't have to be frightened we'll laugh at him if he suddenly says something stupid.'

'He won't be tongue-tied with strangers for much longer,' said Lizzie. 'There's nothing wrong with him that a few conquests won't cure.'

'Then let's hope he has some luck with Arabella this evening,' Sophy said.

'Yes,' said Jane. 'It'll make him feel much more comfortable. Oh dear,' she went on, turning to Lizzie. 'Here's Lord Beveridge. I think he wants to dance with you.'

'Oh, no,' sighed Lizzie, turning towards Lord Beveridge who was creating havoc as he walked across the drawing-room. He bumped into an elderly dowager before tripping over a débutante and then knocking into a footman, sending the poor man flying and spilling his tray of champagne. 'He's the clumsiest person I've ever met. He'll step on my hem if he stands next to me, just like the last time, and I won't dare move, because if I do my dress will be torn to shreds.'

'If you want to make your escape we'll cover for you,' said Sophy. 'We'll tell him your mother wanted you.'

'It's too late for that,' said Lizzie, 'I'll have to brave it.'

She looked heavenwards as Lord Beveridge joined her, but she smiled politely all the same. If only she'd been sensible she could have gone to Lady

Hansdowne's ball instead!

'How did everything go last night?'

Lizzie was sitting in Sandy's drawing-room the following morning and Miss Withershanks, her companion, was with them as well. Lizzie should really have waited until the afternoon to see Sandy, it would have been much more the thing, but even though she'd had a late night she was as fresh as a daisy and she didn't want to wait.

Sandy was always up early too. It had got them into a lot of trouble when they'd been children. They'd kept going on fishing expeditions before anyone else was awake, or riding expeditions, or any other kind of expeditions they could think of, and they still did the same when they were in the country.

'Do you want the good news or the bad news?' he asked her.

'Miss Withershanks,' said Lizzie, turning to her companion, 'Lord Masterson has some very nice engravings, would you like to look at them?'

'Oh, yes, please,' Miss Withershanks said.

Lizzie sat Miss Withershanks at the far side of the room with the engravings then she settled down for a good gossip with Sandy.

'I want to hear the good news,' she said firmly.

'The good news is the evening started very well. Arabella looked like an angel.'

Lizzie made herself listen to a description of Arabella's beauty by reminding herself that Sandy had listened to her when she had thought she was in love with Lord Hanson a few months ago. He hadn't even laughed when she'd said Lord Hanson looked like a young Adonis.

'She was wearing the prettiest white muslin gown,' said Sandy, 'showing all her -' He stopped and coughed. 'Yes, well, and her hair had the loveliest little ringlets arranged round her face. When I went into the ballroom she looked at me and she smiled.'

'Goodness,' said Lizzie. 'What happened next?'

'Next she fluttered her fan in front of her face, then she fluttered her eyelashes, then she smiled again, I thought I'd died and gone to heaven. Then she started walking towards me.'

'Goodness,' said Lizzie again. Somehow she hadn't expected Arabella to like Sandy, Arabella usually liked wicked men not countrified people like Sandy.

'Then she smiled again,' said Sandy.

'She seems to have been doing a lot of smiling,' Lizzie remarked.

'She looked wonderful,' said Sandy. 'She walked closer and closer, swinging her hips, and all the time she was flirting with her fan . . . and then she walked straight past me.'

'Oh no!' said Lizzie.

'Oh yes. I turned round to see where she was going, and she was walking straight towards Wrexham. It was him she'd been smiling at all along.'

'Oh dear,' sighed Lizzie.

Still, it was not surprising, Lord Wrexham was the handsomest man in London. His dark hair hung below his collar and it made him look like a pirate. His black eyes were always smouldering and he was always leaning carelessly against things, mostly walls and pillars. His clothes clung to all his muscles and made all the ladies want to cling to him as well.

'Why do women always fall in love with rakes?' asked Sandy in exasperation. 'Wrexham's reputation is enough to send any normal person running away from him, but women are drawn to him like moths to a flame. He's a gambler, he's a wastrel, he fights, he's had a string of mistresses - all at once, not one at a time like anyone else - and he's even supposed to have been a smuggler. I can't understand it.' He turned his brown eyes towards her. 'Can you?'

Be nice, she told herself. 'No.'

'You're lying' he said accusingly. I can always tell. Your eyebrows go up at the sides when you lie.'

'Do they?' she asked in astonishment.

'Yes.'

'I never knew that. Have you always known - when I've been lying, I mean.'

'Always.'

'That time when I took Aries out?' she asked, remembering the time she'd been caught riding Sandy's devilish horse. She'd been too scared to admit she'd taken it because she knew she shouldn't have been riding it, so she'd pretended she'd found Aries wandering in the fields and had said she'd led him home as a kindness.

'Yes.'

'But you didn't say anything.'

'You were only fourteen. I should have been cross with you, I suppose, but I was impressed.'

'You were?'

'Of course I was, anyone who can handle a horse

like that is a heck of a rider, especially if she is a girl.'

'And here I've been all these years, thinking you believed every word I said!'

'But that's not the point,' said Sandy. 'The point is: why does Arabella like Wrexham? And, more to the point: why does she prefer him to me?'

'Stupidity,' said Lizzie loyally.

'Your eyes flashed, too.'

'Hm?' she asked him innocently.

'When I mentioned Wrexham's name your eyes flashed, so what is it? I'm relying on you to tell me the secret, Lizzie, why do women always fall in love with rakes?'

She was thoughtful. 'Do you know, I'm not sure, other than the obvious, that is.'

'The obvious?'

'Yes, you know, the way you start thinking -' She stopped suddenly.

'The way you start thinking what?'

'Oh, nothing,' she said hurriedly.

'I thought you were meant to be helping me,' he said, looking hurt.

'I am.'

'Then tell me, what's the obvious?'

'Well . . . ' She squirmed. This was going to be difficult. Or maybe not. 'Why do men like women like Arabella?' she asked.

'Isn't it obv - Oh.' He stopped short. 'I see what you mean.' Then he frowned. 'You mean that when you look at Wrexham you start thinking about -'

'Never mind what I start thinking about,' said Lizzie hurriedly. 'Apart from the obvious, that's what we were talking about, not the obvious, and I suggest we stick to it.'

'Well?' he asked.

'Well.' She stopped. 'Do you know, now I come to think about it, I don't know. It seems ridiculous. You're right, his reputation ought to send women running away, but it does quite the opposite. I'll have to ask the girls.'

'Are Jane and Sophy in town?'

'Yes. They missed you last night. I told them you were . . . otherwise engaged.'

'Getting humiliated,' he said ruefully.

'Oh, well, look on the bright side, it could have been worse, at least you didn't start talking to her. As far as she's concerned you never thought she was smiling at you in the first place.'

He looked at her innocently. 'You were saying?'

'Oh no,' she laughed.

'As soon as she was close enough I said, "Miss Wentworth, I can't believe this is happening, you're the most beautiful girl I've ever seen in my life. I didn't know you'd be interested in - " and that was as far as I got before she sailed straight past me as thought I didn't even exist.'

'Poor Sandy! Never mind, are you coming to Lady Ibbotson's card party this evening?'

He sighed. 'I suppose so.'

'Good, the girls will be there, so this afternoon we'll see if we can decide why women fall in love with rakes and let you know this evening.' She stood up. It was time for her to go. 'Miss Withershanks?' she said.

Miss Withershanks closed the book of engravings and stood up as well.

Lizzie kissed Sandy on the cheek, whilst Miss Withershanks said: 'Well, really,' because she thought it was far too forward, even though Lizzie and Sandy had known each other since they were little children. Then the butler showed them out of the house. It was time for Lizzie to go home for lunch, and then she was going to see the girls.

Chapter Two

'There you are,' said Lizzie's mother as she met Lizzie in the hall, 'I was beginning to wonder where you'd got to. Where have you been?'

'I've been to see Sandy -'

'I might have known it,' said her mother with a sigh. 'You're always going to see Sandy. But really, Lizzie, you know you're meant to wait until the afternoon. I hope you remembered to take Miss Withershanks with you.'

'Of course I did.'

'Well, I suppose that's something, but there's no time for talking now. Hurry up and take off your outdoor things and then go into the drawing-room. Lord Beveridge is here and he is waiting to speak to you.'

'Lord Beveridge?' Lizzie's heart sank. 'What does he want?'

'Really, Lizzie, to pay his addresses to you, of course, what else would he want?'

'Mother, you haven't given him permission?' asked Lizzie in dismay.

'What kind of mother would I be if I hadn't? Of course I've given him permission. It's time you stopped being so fussy, Lizzie, and made up your mind to settle down. You're not a girl any more, you know, you're twenty-three, and if you're not careful you'll end up on the shelf.'

'But Lord Beveridge . . . ' Lizzie protested.

'There's nothing wrong with Lord Beveridge.

He's a very good catch. He's wealthy, and he's titled and he's even rather nice looking. He might not be the brightest star in the firmament but he's not an imbecile, and in such a long-established family that's by no means to be sneezed at. If you take my advice you'll encourage him. It won't be difficult, it will only need a smile and a couple of kind words to bring him up to scratch, then you can be married at the end of the season. Just think, you could be Lady Beveridge by July.'

'Perish the thought,' shuddered Lizzie. 'I can't think of anything worse.'

'Here,' said her mother impatiently, starting to untie the strings of Lizzie's bonnet in an effort to get her ready more quickly. 'Let me help you off with your bonnet. We've spent so long chattering you don't have time to go upstairs any more. You'll just have to get out of your outdoor things down here.'

Lizzie knew she couldn't talk her mother out of her plans and she knew she'd have to go through with them anyway, so she decided she might as well get her interview with Lord Beveridge over with as quickly as possible. She took off her bonnet and slipped out of her pelisse and then she went through into the drawing-room, where Lord Beveridge was standing over by the window.

Oh, Lord! thought Lizzie, it's impossible. There's absolutely no way I can marry him.

'Miss Carstairs.' Lord Beveridge beamed at her, then coughed nervously and said her name again. 'Miss Carstairs.'

'Lord Beveridge. Won't you sit down?' Lizzie's manners, when pushed, were impeccable, and at this moment they were very pushed, but even her mother wouldn't have found any fault with the way she was treating her unwanted suitor.

'Miss Carstairs,' said Lord Beveridge, and cleared his throat again.

'Would you like something to drink?' asked Lizzie. She didn't know whether he was coughing because he was nervous, or whether he was suffering from a sore throat, but either way she thought offering him a drink might make things easier for him.

'A drink?' he asked in surprise.

'For your cough.'

'Oh.' He looked startled. 'Oh, no thank you. Miss Carstairs,' he began again, but this time he spoke with what Lizzie had an alarming feeling was meant to be passion. She had the sudden feeling that her mother had played her a dastardly turn. Her heart was in her mouth as she realized that Lord Beveridge hadn't just called to pay her his addresses, he'd called to offer her his hand.

'My dear Miss Carstairs, you must let me tell you that ever since the first moment I saw you I've worshipped the very ground you walk on,' said Lord Beveridge, suddenly dropping to one knee and putting his hands on his heart.

'Goodness,' said Lizzie, not knowing what else to say, then adding, 'but it was only a week last Tuesday, you know.'

'You're the most beautiful goddess I've ever seen in my life,' he went on, taking no notice of her protest. It was rather odd for a worshipper, thought Lizzie, because worshippers might generally be expected to listen to their goddess, if only to find out how the goddess would like to be worshipped, and to avoid being smited – or should that be smoted? - by a thunderbolt for not paying attention.

But Lord Beveridge was continuing. 'The . . . the most . . . ' He stopped and glanced at his palm then he went on, 'the most bewitching creature, and I can't rest until I make you . . . ' he glanced at his hand again. ' . . . dash it all,' he muttered. Before finishing: ' . . . until I make you my life.'

'Are you sure that should be life? Shouldn't it be wife?' asked Lizzie curiously.

He looked at his hand again and frowned. 'Ever since I saw you,' he muttered, rapidly repeating his speech under his breath, 'dah-de-dah-de-dah . . . make you . . . I think it should be wife,' he said out loud. Well?' he asked, getting up off his knees, 'what do you think?'

'I'm honoured you think me worthy of such a proposal,' said Lizzie, making sure she kept a straight face. 'It's very kind of you, and I'm sure I'm very flattered, but I'm afraid I must refuse.'

He groaned. 'Now I'll have to do it all over again with Miss Everton instead. I'm not looking forward to it, I can tell you, she's got a laugh like a hyena and she looks like a horse.' He looked at Lizzie wistfully. 'Perhaps if I try again another day?'

'No, I'm afraid not,' said Lizzie, shaking her head.

'Are you sure you won't change your mind?'
'Absolutely positive.'
'Oh, well then, it can't be helped. Don't bother to ring for the butler, I'll show myself out.'

He left the room and as soon as he'd gone, her

mother entered it. 'Well?' she asked. 'From the look on his face I suppose you turned him down?'

'You knew he was going to propose to me,' said Lizzie accusingly.

'Of course I knew he was going to propose to you. I also knew it would be impossible to get you into the drawing-room if you knew it, too. You can't go on turning people down for ever, though, Lizzie. If you don't get married this season I'm not sure I'll be willing to come to London again. I'm not as young as I was and it gets more tiring every year.'

'You love coming to London,' said Lizzie, 'that's just a ruse on your part to get me to say yes to the next person that offers for me. You know as well as I do that you'd be bored to death at home, especially in the winter. There's nothing to do in the country in the winter. You're always saying so.'

'That's as may be, but I want to get you off my hands before the end of the year, or I might never have another chance, and you might never have another chance of catching a husband, either. That's why we've come to London early this year. It isn't that I don't like having you at home, but it's time you were married, and Sophy and Jane too. You three girls are fast becoming settled spinsters, you don't want to end up like Miss Withershanks.'

'I'll never end up like Miss Withershanks,' said Lizzie, kissing her mother on the cheek. 'I'd never be content to sit still, looking at engravings. If I end up a spinster then I'll chase the footmen round the house in my bath chair.'

'Lizzie, what will you say next?' said her mother, but she was laughing. 'Just think about what I've said though, my dear.'

'I will,' said Lizzie. 'Now, let's go in to lunch.'

'Why do women like rakes?'

Lizzie was sitting on Sophy's bed, and she asked the girls the question that Sandy had asked her that morning.

Sophy and Jane, who were busy doing each other's hair in new and interesting styles, frowned.

'What's brought that on?' asked Jane.

'Sandy.'

'You've seen him?' she asked.

'Yes, I went round to his house this morning to see how he got on at Lady Hansdowne's ball.'

'And?' asked Sophy.

'He got on very well . . . to begin with, that is. Arabella flirted with him across the room, she smiled and fluttered her eyelashes and wafted her fan.'

'Arabella fluttered her eyelashes at Sandy?' asked Sophy.

'It's a hoax, it's a dream,' said Jane. 'It has to be.'

'That's right, spoil the surprise! All right, I admit it, she didn't smile at Sandy, he just thought she did. He'd really got his hopes up, she walked towards him, still simpering and flirting . . . and then she walked straight past him, and went over to Lord Wrexham instead.'

'Wrexham?' gasped Jane.

'Wrexham was there?' asked Sophy breathlessly.

They both spoke together.

'Yes, which was good news for Arabella, and bad news for Sandy, because she didn't want to look at anyone else, and that's what made Sandy ask me why women are attracted to rakes.'

'Apart from the obvious?' asked Jane.

'Apart from the fact they make your knees tremble and your heart pound and your mouth go dry?' quizzed Sophy.

'Apart from that,' said Lizzie firmly. 'Sandy's right, Wrexham's reputation is enough to make any sane person steer clear of him but he's got women falling over themselves to get near him. He only has to walk into a room and every female head turns to look, before having a daydream about him sweeping them into his arms and kissing them passionately to death.'

The girls were thoughtful. They were asking themselves the question: why did women like rakes?

'It's the way they look,' said Sophy, after a while.

'The way they stand,' said Jane.

'The way they smoulder,' added Sophy.

'The way they make you feel inside,' said Jane.

By now the two girls were well on their way and it would take brute force to stop them coming up with a hundred and one more reasons for why women liked rakes. Lizzie didn't want to stop them, because this was what Sandy wanted to know.

'Yes, but what is it about the way they look?' asked Lizzie. 'It's not just that they're handsome. Wrexham is, but there are other rakes who aren't, in fact Denholme's downright ugly.'

'It's not the way they look, exactly, but more the way they look,' said Sophy. 'What I mean is,' she said, seeing Jane's rolling eyes, 'it's not their appearance, it's more the way they look at everyone else, as though everyone else is beneath their notice.'

'Yes,' nodded Jane. 'It's the way they look down on everyone, as though they're better than everyone else.'

'But why should that make us like them?' mused Lizzie. 'It doesn't make sense.'

'It's because we have to prove them wrong,' suggested Sophy. 'Our pride is at stake, we can't let them dismiss us as nothing, we have to make them see we're something, and until we do, we can't stop trying.'

'It could be,' said Lizzie thoughtfully, 'but I've always thought it's because we can't have them.'

Jane and Sophy raised their eyebrows.

'Not as lovers,' said Lizzie with a mischievous smile. 'We might be able to have them as lovers, if we were so lost to all decorum as to fall for their wicked ways, that is, but we can't have them as our friends or our husbands, because they're not interested in that kind of thing, so it makes us want them. You always want what you can't have.'

'Maybe it's even simpler than that. Maybe we know they'll never settle down, so we know it's safe for us to be besotted with them because they'll never try to make us settle down either,' said Sophy.

Lizzie shifted uncomfortably. Talk of settling down reminded her of Lord Beveridge and his proposal.

'Out with it,' said Jane accusingly. 'Something's happened that you're not telling us about.'

Lizzie sighed. 'It's only that Beveridge proposed this morning.'

'Lord Beveridge proposed?' echoed Sophy. 'Oh,

heavens!'

'I know,' grinned Lizzie.

'What did you say?'

'What I always say, of course. I thanked him for his kind offer but told him I had to refuse.'

'How did he take it?'

'He was upset, but only because he'd have to propose to Miss Everton instead.'

'He didn't say that?'

Jane and Sophy collapsed into laughter.

'He did, and not only that, he had his speech written on the palm of his hand and he kept looking at it to remind himself what to say; which would have been a good idea, but the ink had run and instead of asking me to be his wife, he asked me to be his life.'

Jane and Sophy giggled again.

'Where are the real men?' said Sophy. 'The ones who make up passionate proposals on the spur of the moment and then kill themselves if we refuse to marry them?'

'I shouldn't like that,' said Jane with a frown.

'Me neither,' said Sophy truthfully. 'That's what's so disappointing, the things that are such fun in daydreams would be awful in real life.'

'They would, and that brings us back to why we like rakes,' said Lizzie. 'If we follow your theory we should only like them in daydreams, but we don't, we like them in real life too, even though they drink and gamble and womanise. Why is that?'

They fell silent.

'It's a mystery,' said Sophy.

'That's not good enough,' said Lizzie. 'I promised Sandy I'd find out and explain it to him. He wants to know what he's doing wrong.'

'Sandy's adorable just the way he is,' said Sophy. 'Any woman who doesn't see that needs her head examining.'

'Well of course he is, I told him that,' said Lizzie, 'but he wouldn't listen. Arabella doesn't find him adorable, and right now that's all he cares about.'

'He's better off without her.'

'I know that, and you know that, but I don't see how we can convince him of that.'

'He'll find out soon enough,' said Jane.

Lizzie sighed. 'I hope so.'

Sophy paused. 'You weren't tempted?' she asked.

'By what?' asked Lizzie, startled.

'Beveridge.'

Lizzie laughed.

'We're not getting any younger,' Jane pointed out.

'That's just what my mother said!' remarked Lizzie.

'She's right, though, we're not,' said Jane, 'and if we don't get married - well, what else is there for us?'

It was a sobering thought. The choices facing them were almost non-existent. They could either get married or they could become old maids.

'Even so, I'm not getting married just because there isn't anything else to do,' said Lizzie firmly. 'We might not be allowed to run mills or join the army or do any of the things the men are allowed to do, but I'm still not going to marry someone like Beveridge just to have a ring on my finger. If I have to, then I'll die an old maid.'

Jane pulled a face. 'That would be horrid,

everyone would laugh at you.'

'No they wouldn't, Miss Austen is right,' said Sophy, who had just finished reading Miss Austen's Emma and loved every minute of it. 'A single woman with a large fortune will never be ridiculous.'

'That's not really fair,' remarked Lizzie.

'I know, but that's the way it is,' said Jane. 'So let's be thankful we each have a fortune and we don't have to accept the offers of men like Beveridge to keep us respectable.'

'Besides, I don't see what's so bad about being on the shelf,' said Lizzie. 'Without a husband we can do as we please and we don't have to take orders from someone else.'

'I agree. I would hate it if I had a husband who was always telling me what to do,' said Sophy.

Lizzie raised an imaginary glass. 'To spinsterhood,' she said.

'To spinsterhood,' said Jane and Sophy. 'May it go on for ever!'

Chapter Three

There were lots of people at Lady Ibbotson's card party but it was not a crush as the season proper had not yet begun. Lizzie had no trouble in making out Sandy at the far side of the room. He was being monopolised by the Honourable Mrs Dawson, a buxom widow whose laugh rang out over the assembly like a clarion bell. Sandy was running his finger round the inside of his collar in agitation. He was too polite to leave Mrs Dawson, even though he found her completely overpowering, but as soon as he spotted Lizzie his expression pleaded for help.

Lizzie went over to his side, telling the Honourable Mrs Dawson that she would have to whisk Lord Partington away as he had promised to fetch her an ice, and she would expire if he didn't get her one.

'Brazen hussy,' declared Mrs Dawson as Lizzie led Sandy away.

Sandy himself said: 'Thank goodness for that, Lizzie! I thought I'd never escape.'

'What you need are some good excuses, then you won't be trapped again,' Lizzie told him.

'They wouldn't have done me any good with the Honourable Mrs Dawson. I kept opening my mouth, but then I kept having to shut it again, I couldn't get a word in edgeways. If only Arabella would monopolise me like that,' he said, with a yearning glance in the blonde beauty's direction. Then he turned to Lizzie with enquiring eyes. 'You were going to tell me why women fall head over heels for rakes. I hope you haven't forgotten.'

'No, of course not.' She gave his arm a squeeze. 'I've been talking to the girls but we can't agree, Sophy thinks it's the way they look down on everyone, Jane thinks it's the way they stand, draping themselves negligently against pillars, and all three of us think it's the way they smoulder.'

'And?'

'And what?'

'That's it? They way they look down on people, they way they stand and the way they smoulder?' He caught sight of Lord Denholme, another well-known rake, who was being gazed at longingly by a dozen young ladies. 'If that's all there is to it I should master it in no time.'

'Of course you will,' said Lizzie, taking his arm.

'With a pat on the head,' said Sandy.

She looked at him in surprise. 'What on earth do you mean by that?'

'I mean that if you're going to use that tone of voice, you might as well go the whole way and pat me on the head whilst you're about it,' he said irritably.

'I don't know what you're talking about,' she protested.

'I'm talking about you soothing me as though I'm still in leading strings. You'd never use that tone of voice to Wrexham, would you?' he said as he led her over to one of the card tables. Sandy wasn't fond of cards but as it was a card party he'd just have to grin and bear it.

'Well . . . ' began Lizzie.

He raised his eyebrows.

'Well, all right then, now you mention it, no, I wouldn't use that tone of voice to Wrexham.'

'You see what I mean? You don't take me seriously, and it's not just you. I love you dearly -'

'You do?' she asked in surprise.

'Of course I do,' he said, giving her an affectionate hug. 'But I'm getting tired of women not taking me seriously.'

'Yes, I can see that you might.'

'And it's all because I don't look at people the right way, stand right and smoulder,' he said. 'If I did all those things, would women start to take me seriously?'

She thought about it.

'Well?' he asked.

'I'm not sure,' she said cautiously. No matter how Sandy looked at other people, or stood either for that matter, she couldn't imagine him managing to smoulder, and even if he did . . . she took in his chubby figure, his countrified clothes, and sighed. 'I'm afraid there's more to it than that.'

'I thought there must be, otherwise everyone would be doing it. Even so, it's a place to start. Lizzie, I've come to a decision. I want to become a rake.'

She looked at him in astonishment, pausing halfway along the row of chairs.

'Not a real rake. Not drinking and gambling and womanising,' he corrected himself hastily.

'I should hope not indeed!' she said in outraged tones.

'But the rest of it. I want women to notice me.

Not the likes of the Honourable Mrs Dawson,' he said, as he caught sight of the elderly woman, who was squeezed into a muslin gown more suited to someone twenty years younger and twenty pounds lighter, and who was waving to him from the other side of the room. 'But the likes of —'

'Arabella Wentworth?'

'That would be nice. Oh, I know it's probably not realistic to begin with, ' he admitted. 'I dare say I'd have to get some practise in first, but yes, in the end, Arabella. I want her to sail across a room to me, ignoring every other man in her path, just like she did to Wrexham.'

'You want her to simper and flirt with you?' asked Lizzie. Her voice showed what she thought of this kind of behaviour.

Sandy grinned.

It took Lizzie by surprise. There was something almost wolfish about it. Goodness! she thought. I didn't know he had it in him, she looked at him thoughtfully because it made him look quite different.

'Yes, I do. Well?' he asked, as he handed Lizzie into her seat, 'what do you say? Will you help me?'

She sat down. Then she sighed. 'I don't want to disappoint you, Sandy, but I don't think it's possible. You're just too nice to be a rake.'

He looked hurt. 'I can learn to be nasty.'

'I dare say you can, but what's the point?' She smiled at him sincerely as the cards were cut. 'There's no need for you to change yourself, I like you just the way you are.'

'I know,' he said morosely. 'But you're not Arabella.'

Lizzie's face fell. No, she was forced to admit it, she wasn't Arabella.

'A rake? Sandy?' Sophy giggled the following afternoon, when the three girls met up at Hookham's lending library, one of their favourite rendezvous.
'Why not?' Lizzie had been convinced it was a ridiculous idea as well but as soon as Sophy started giggling she stuck up for Sandy.
'Oh, Lizzie, Sandy could never be a rake in a million years, he's far too nice.'
'He doesn't want to be a rake, he just wants to look like one, not behave like one. And really, you know, it isn't that far fetched.'
'We all know how much you like him,' said Jane. 'We do, too. But he'll never look like Wrexham or Denholme.'
'I don't see why not,' said Lizzie. By now she was determined to convince the others. 'He's tall, he has a broad chest and broad shoulders -'
'But he's plump!'
'He isn't plump,' said Lizzie, taking a book from the shelves. 'He's cuddly.'
'That's what I mean!' said Sophy. 'Rakes aren't cuddly. They're long and lean, like panthers.'
'Or like jaguars,' put in Jane, getting into the spirit of things.
'Or like tigers, prowling through the jungle.'
Lizzie looked heavenward. 'Panthers and jaguars and tigers I'll grant you, I'll even give you prowling, but not even Wrexham can manage a jungle. He has to make do with ballrooms and drawing-rooms like everyone else.'

'Maybe so, but he still looks as though he belongs in the jungle,' sighed Sophy.

'Sandy could look as though he belonged in a jungle,' said Lizzie. The girls were looking at her pityingly. 'He just needs a bit of practise, that's all.'

Jane shook her head. 'It's a nice idea but it wouldn't work, and what's more you know it.'

Lizzie sighed. 'There must be something we can do to help him. How are we going to get him noticed by Arabella?'

They thought.

'Does it have to be Arabella?' asked Sophy, 'or could it be Camilla Ridgeley? She's very pretty, but she's very young, and she'll like the fact that Sandy's an earl. She'll be flattered he's taken an interest in her and she'll be eager to please.'

Lizzie shook her head. 'He doesn't want Camilla, he wants Arabella, and I want to help him get her.'

Sophy and Jane looked at her in surprise.

'If he could win her affections he'd soon discover she's spoilt,' Lizzie explained. 'Then he could move on to more deserving girls. And it would do him so much good. If he could win Arabella's devotion he would know he could win anyone's attention, and he'd never have to be tongue-tied or embarrassed in female company again.'

'You've got a point,' said Sophy.

Jane agreed. 'That's the one thing wrong with the season, there's no real chance to get to know people, which is a bad thing as far as Sandy's concerned. Once he gets to know someone he starts to relax with them and then he's fun to be with, but until then . . . '

All three of them thought of a number of painful

episodes in the past when Sandy had been so tongue-tied in the presence of a young lady that he had barely been able to push three words out, or if he had managed to speak he had gone on to say something ever so dull.

'Are you sure we couldn't do it?' asked Sophy, biting her bottom lip. 'Turn him into a rake, I mean?'

Jane gave it serious consideration. 'It's possible, I suppose.'

Lizzie said, 'It's worth a try.'

A glare from the librarian told them they needed to choose their books more quietly, and they spent the next ten minutes choosing some Gothic romances to read. Then when they'd chosen their books, they left the library and started to walk back home.

'We could always spread some false rumours about his past,' said Sophy thoughtfully, returning to the subject of Sandy. 'That should help him. It would give him an air of mystery.'

Jane was impressed. 'That's a good idea, but it would have to be a scandalous past.'

'No one looking at Sandy would believe he had a scandalous past,' objected Lizzie as they crossed the road.

'Not now, but when we've turned him into a rake they would. After all, that's the whole point of the exercise.'

'That's true,' said, narrowly avoiding a brewer's cart. 'But can we do it?' She lost confidence a bit as she thought of how big the problem was, and what they had to do.

Sophy frowned. 'We'll have to look him over and see,' she said.

'Yes, we will,' Jane agreed.

'You'll have to invite him round to your house, Lizzie, tomorrow afternoon, and we'll have a good look at him and see if it can be done,' said Sophy.

'All right, but no laughing, this is a serious business, if we take it on we can't let Sandy down.'

They had come to a stop outside Lizzie's house. The girls looked suitably serious.

'Very well,' Lizzie said. 'I have high hopes of tomorrow. If we all pull together we can help him catch Arabella.'

Chapter Four

'We've decided to do it.'

'Do what?' asked Sandy cautiously.

'Turn you into a rake.'

Lizzie had paid a visit to Sandy's house and was telling him about their plan.

'The girls are coming over to my house this afternoon and you're going to join us. We're going to look you over and see if it can be done.'

'Anything Wrexham can do,' said Sandy.

'It's no good trying to run before you can walk.' Lizzie looked at him critically. 'You'd better not set your sights on being another Wrexham just yet. Sophy thinks we should spread some false rumours about you, to give you a dangerous or scandalous past. It will make you seem more interesting.'

'Is that a good idea?'

'Of course it is. Women love a man with something dangerous in his past, it gives them something to think about. It's even better if it's a secret because then they have to try and work it out.'

'It had better not be too scandalous, though. I wouldn't want to upset my grandmother.'

Lizzie sighed. 'She's a perfect dear, and you're a perfect dear for thinking about her, but you mustn't go saying that kind of thing to any other young lady if you want to be taken for a rake.'

'Why not?' he asked.

'Because it doesn't work. Rakes don't care about their grandmothers, they don't care about anyone, except of course, the young woman they're talking to. Or at least that's what she hopes. But even she has the disturbing idea he doesn't care about her either, which keeps her on edge and interested. It's all part of being like a jungle cat.'

'A jungle cat?' Sandy sounded surprised and then alarmed.

'Yes, you must have noticed it, all rakes have it, a sort of air of being like a wild animal prowling through the jungle, needing no one, entirely alone.'

'Have you gone mad?' asked Sandy mildly. 'I only ask, because if you have I know a very good doctor who's used to dealing with this sort of thing.'

'Trust me,' said Lizzie, 'rakes are always like jungle animals. They're hard and predatory and once they've seen their quarry they stalk their prey.'

'You have gone mad.'

'In fact, you could practise now,' said Lizzie, ignoring his humorous comment and getting on with the matter in hand. She stood up and moved the furniture, pushing the chaise longue to one side of the room and the group of Heppelwhite chairs to the other to make a space down the middle of the room. 'Go over to the door and then come into the room, pretending to be a panther.'

Sandy looked at her for a moment and then said, 'No. I don't mind changing the way I look and I'll even smoulder like a volcano if I have to, but I draw the line at trying to walk like a panther.'

'Like a tiger then, or a jaguar, or any other wild cat you care to name. Do it for Arabella,' she said encouragingly.

Sandy had looked like he was about to throw the

whole scheme into the air, but when Lizzie reminded him what he was doing it for he said, 'Oh, all right, if I must, but don't blame me if I make a complete fool of myself.'

He walked over to the door and then turned round, dropping to his hands and knees.

Lizzie was aghast. 'What are you doing?' she asked in horror.

'What do you think I'm doing?' he asked peevishly. 'I'm pretending to be a panther.'

'Not like that! When have you ever seen Wrexham walking into a room like that?'

'I knew it was ridiculous,' grumbled Sandy, picking himself up and dusting off his breeches. 'I told you so at the time.'

'I didn't mean you to get down on all fours, I meant you to walk into the room like this,' Lizzie explained. She went over to the door and walked sinuously into the room, casting disdainful glances around her to left and right.

'I can't do that, I'll look like an utter coxcomb,' he said in horror.

'Try.' She pushed him into place, grumbling that he felt ridiculous, then he tried to copy the way she'd walked into the room.

She clapped her hand over her eyes, not knowing whether to laugh or cry. 'Yes, well, I think we'll leave that until later,' she said, trying to blot out the picture of Sandy swinging into the room like an aging roué suffering from gout. 'First things first, you're to come to my house tomorrow and the girls and I will look you over and decide if it can be done.'

'It can be done,' said Sandy determinedly, 'and

what's more, I intend to do it. If you and the girls don't help me, I'll just have to do it myself.'

'Don't mention panthers,' Lizzie said to Sophy and Jane as they waited for Sandy to arrive on the following afternoon.
'But it's all part of the plan,' Sophy said.
'Maybe, but he's not ready for it yet. We want to concentrate on how he looks and what he's wearing and see if we can't come up with a few simple ways of making him look more like a rake. We can leave the difficult things until later.'
'I agree,' said Jane. 'We don't even know if we can do it yet.'
'We have to,' said Lizzie firmly. 'Sandy's going to do it with or without our help, he told me so himself, so we have to make sure we do everything we possibly can to help him. Otherwise, who knows what the results will be?'
There came the noise of someone arriving in the hall below and a few minutes later Sandy was shown into the drawing room.
'Sandy!' Sophy and Jane were delighted to see him. They all lived in neighbouring villages in the pretty county of Cambridgeshire and had grown up together, so that they were all friends.
'Sophy. Jane,' he greeted them. 'You're here too. Good, Lizzie said you would be. In that case, I can't fail.'
The three girls looked at each other. It was nice that he believed in them but his entrance hadn't been encouraging for the task they had in hand. He had sauntered into the room like a schoolboy and had then

perched on the edge of a damasked sofa. They were used to seeing him doing this sort of thing. But all that would have to change if he was to become a rake. Rakes didn't perch on the edge of sofas, they threw themselves carelessly onto any piece of furniture that happened to be available and gazed cynically at the world at large, but that kind of detail would have to wait until later. Right now it was his clothes they wanted to put right.

All three of them stared at him critically.

'If only I could get this much attention from Arabella,' he joked.

'You will,' Lizzie reassured him.

Oh no! she was doing it again - reassuring him. Oh well, old habits died hard. Still, that was all about to change.

'You'll need to do something with your hair,' said Sophy. She looked at him earnestly with her head on one side. 'It needs to be longer and wilder, it should fall down on to your collar, instead of being cut so short.'

'Yes,' agreed Jane. Her eyes were half closed as she looked at him as well. 'You'll have to stop going to your barber, your hair's too neat and trimmed.'

'But the Brutus is all the rage,' protested Sandy, defending his hairstyle, which was one of the most popular hairstyles of the day. 'Everyone's wearing their hair this way.'

'No, they're not,' said Lizzie. 'Not the rakes. The girls are right. You have to change your hair.' She went over to him and rearranged it, pulling it down at the sides to see the effect. It felt good between her fingers, silky and smooth. 'It will suit you longer. It makes your face seem thinner, and it brings out your cheekbones. You know,' she went on thoughtfully, 'you've got very good bones . . .'

'At last! I'm glad I've got something that's all right!'

'But there's too much fat on them.'

'What do you mean, there's too much fat on them!' He pushed himself out of the chair and crossed to the mirror. He looked at himself closely. 'Nonsense. I don't want to look like a scarecrow.'

Jane and Sophy agreed with Lizzie. 'Too much fat.'

Sandy didn't look pleased, but he shrugged. 'If you say so.'

'You could really do with losing weight all over,' said Lizzie.

'Is this being cruel to be kind?' joked Sandy.

'You're the one who wanted to be a rake,' she reminded him.

'I must have been mad, but go on.'

'Well, the truth is you're too much of a roly poly to be a rake, you need to take more exercise. But don't worry, you should have time to trim down nicely before the season proper begins.'

He sat down again, this time on the seat of the sofa. 'But I already get plenty of exercise. I go riding, I work out at Gentleman Jackson's gym, and I fence.'

'Even so, you'll have to start doing it more often, and stop eating so many of Anatole's cakes. He's too good a chef, it makes you eat more than you should and then you get cuddly instead of lean. You'll have to get rid of him.'

'No.' Sandy put his foot down. 'I'm not getting

rid of Anatole, he's the best chef I've ever had. His grape pudding is one of the most wonderful things I've ever eaten.'

Lizzie put her hands on her hips. 'Do you want to be a rake or not?'

'And his soufflés are as light as a feather,' said Sandy obstinately.

'And Arabella?' asked Lizzie.

He wrestled with himself for a minute. 'All right, you win.' He grumbled under his breath. 'But if I have to get rid of Anatole, you have to get rid of calling me Sandy. From now on, I'm Alex.'

Lizzie agreed.

But Alex was still grumbling when he left, saying, 'This is going to be a lot harder than I thought.'

Chapter Five

Alex went back to his London house and threw his hat on a chair. 'I must be mad,' he said to his reflection as he peered at himself in the mirror. Am I really plump? he wondered. He ran his hands over his face, then he turned sideways to see if he had a paunch. Hmm, he wasn't exactly fat but he wasn't lean and mean either. Lean and mean. He grinned. He liked the thought of that.

He held in his stomach and pulled a rakish scowl, then he sighed. His rakish scowl looked more like he was suffering from indigestion, but he was determined to go ahead with his scheme. He was tired of women treating him like a much-loved lapdog. He wanted them to look at him as though he was their ideal lover instead.

Take Lizzie, for example. Not that he wanted her looking at him as though he was her ideal lover, far from it! But it would be nice if she would take him a bit more seriously. They'd been inseparable as children, except when he'd been away at school, and they'd gone to local balls and parties together, but she'd never treated him as the older and wiser person he was. In fact, she'd treated him as though he was younger than her. She'd never once asked him for advice.

No, that wasn't quite true, she'd asked his advice about horses and dogs but she'd never asked for his advice on anything important.

He turned it over in his mind. She'd never asked

for his advice on suitable husbands, for instance, and she'd certainly never looked up at him as though he was the fount of all wisdom, which she should have done because he was older than her, and it would have been nice.

It was probably because he wasn't the fount of all wisdom, he reminded himself, but all the same it would have been nice to see some admiration in her eyes, at least once in a while.

Ah, well, that was wishing for the impossible. Lizzie wasn't much for admiring people, and besides, that wasn't what he wanted. What he really wanted was to see admiration in Arabella's eyes instead. He practised another rakish scowl as he thought about Arabella, but this time he didn't make the mistake of looking in the mirror. That way, he wouldn't see what he looked like and could imagine himself looking rakish instead.

The clock chimed the hour. It was time to put all ideas of his transformation out of his head. He was due at his grandmother's in half an hour and he didn't want to be late.

'There you are, my boy,' beamed Alex's grandmother as he walked into her drawing-room. She kissed him on the cheek. 'I've been looking forward to your visit. You're such a good boy for coming to visit me when you're in London, it's not every young man who wants to waste his time on an old woman. They usually want to go out drinking and gambling instead.'

'You're not an old woman. You never seem to age, Grandma, you don't look a day over one-and-twenty.'

'That makes you a miracle baby,' she said with a twinkle in her eye, 'because otherwise I couldn't be a grandmother! But come and sit down. Yes that's right, sit on the other side of the fireplace in the wing chair. I've had it restuffed and it's very comfortable, or so the gentlemen tell me, though I never sit in it myself. I prefer the chaise longue.' She seated herself on the long chair and draped her arm over the single arm rest. 'I'm glad you've been good enough to come and see me. As a reward I've laid on a treat for you. Pierre's spent the morning making your favourite biscuits. Oh! Here they are now, you must have some with your tea.'

The butler set down a silver tray with a teapot, cream jug and sugar bowl on the table next to her, and in the middle of it was a plate of the freshly-baked biscuits.

'Ah.' Alex eyed the biscuits longingly, but then the thought of Arabella flashed through his mind and he stiffened his upper lip. 'I'd love a cup of tea, but I'll have to say no to the biscuits, I'm afraid.'

'Why?' His grandmother was intrigued. 'You never say no to biscuits, are you ill?'

'No, I'm not ill, I just . . . ' Inspiration failed him. What could he say that would satisfy his grandmother? She loved to see him eat, she always had done, ever since he'd been a small boy, and she'd had the biscuits baked specially for him. 'I'm trying to get into a new waistcoat.'

He wouldn't usually say anything of the sort to his grandmother because it would start her asking him if he was seeing a special young lady, then would come questions of who she was, who her family was, and whether he was thinking of making her an offer. But it was the only excuse he could think of that wouldn't hurt her feelings, and besides, more or less, it was the truth.

His grandmother's eyes twinkled. 'Ah! So that's it! At last! Oh, Alex, I'm so pleased.'

'You are?' he asked, trying to pretend he didn't know what she was talking about. There was just a chance he might be able to steer her off the subject if he played the innocent, but he should have known it would be no good.

His grandmother clasped her bony hands. 'It's about time! I've been wanting to see you settled for as long as I can remember. I'm not getting any younger and I want to see my great-grandchildren before I go.'

'It's only a waistcoat,' he said, trying to throw her off the scent.

'There's only one reason you'd care enough about a waistcoat to pass up a chance of one of Pierre's freshly-baked biscuits and that's to impress the woman you love,' she cackled. 'I can't tell you how happy you've made me. I thought you were never going to realize that she was the one.'

'Give me a chance,' laughed Alex. 'I only saw her for the first time last month.'

'Last month?' She looked astounded, then she leant forward and patted his hand, laughing. 'Naughty boy, but I see what you mean, you might have known her all your life, but you've only just seen her. Before that, you took her for granted. Oh, yes, I know exactly what you mean. It was like that with your grandfather and me. I know you don't like to think of it, because we're old people, but we were young once, you know. Of course, I'd known all along we were made for each other, but your grandfather couldn't see it, not until the night of the Heskett's ball. It was the pink satin that did it.' Her eyes became dreamy. 'I thought it might. Your grandfather always did like satin, and he liked me in pink. So what was it for you, my boy? Was it pink satin? Or blue silk? Or white muslin? Or something entirely different? Or did you came across her hitching her stockings up when she thought no one was looking, eh?' she cackled. 'No need to blush, my boy, it wouldn't surprise me if that was it. Lizzie's always been a hoyden, she could never keep her stockings up!'

Lizzie? Lizzie? He nearly laughed out loud. His grandmother must be getting old after all. Funnily enough she still seemed bright as a button but he supposed it had to happen sometime. Lizzie, indeed! Lizzie was pretty enough, and fun to be with, but she was hardly Arabella.

An image of Arabella's white bosom floated before his eyes, and he imagined her saying to him: 'Oh, Alexander, I never dreamed you'd notice me, never mind asking me to marry you. I don't know what to say, I'm overwhelmed.' And her bosom heaved very satisfyingly in Alex's imagination.

But he mustn't disappoint his grandmother by telling her she was wrong about Lizzie. It would be much easier to say nothing about it for the moment. She'd soon come around to the idea once it was definite, but there was no point him saying anything until he knew Arabella was going to be his. It would be too horrible if he told his grandmother all about it and then Arabella didn't want anything to do with him.

But he wasn't going to think about failure, he was going to think about success. He covered up his lack of a reply by taking another drink of tea.

His grandmother didn't notice, though. She didn't need him to reply. As usual, she was talking for both of them. 'It will be a summer wedding, of course, you won't want to wait any longer that that, which means . . . ' She rippled her fingers, as if counting on them, then said ' . . . I'll have my first great-grandchild by the end of April.'

Alex spluttered into his tea. He put down his cup, slopping the tea in the saucer, and tried to stop coughing.

His grandmother cackled again. 'There's no use being coy, my boy, it's what marriage is for, after all, and you don't have to worry about not performing on cue. You'll get her with child on the honeymoon, the Masterson's are a virile lot, the brides always come back from honeymoon enceinte.'

Alex reached for his cup of tea. He was blushing furiously and wanted to hide behind taking another sip. Then he remembered the coughing fit and decided not to bother. Really, his grandmother came out with the most embarrassing things, but she hadn't finished yet.

'It's a lovely time for a baby, April,' she said mistily. 'You can get them outside in the fresh air. There's nothing like a baby kicking its fat arms and legs under a spreading chestnut tree to make you feel all's right with the world, you mark my words. Ah, yes, you've made an old woman very happy. More tea?'

The question took Alex by surprise. He was glad to turn his grandmother's thoughts away from the great-grandchildren he and Lizzie were meant to be producing in time for the following summer, though, so he hurriedly finished the one he had and let her pour him another.

But he should have known better, because now she'd got hold of such an interesting topic of conversation his grandmother wasn't going to let it go.

'So when's the announcement going to be made?' she asked as she put the tea pot back on the silver tray.

'Hold hard, Grandma, you're going too fast.' He couldn't let her go around talking about a wedding between him and Lizzie, what if Lizzie came to hear of it? But he didn't want to explain either. He would have to choose his moment to tell her about Arabella carefully. If not, the old lady might take against her, and if she did that, he wouldn't put it past his grandmother to try and put a spoke in the wheel.

'You're not to say anything about this to anyone,' he said firmly.

She looked surprised. 'What's wrong, haven't you asked her yet, my boy? That's very lax of you. Still, it's kept for twenty years, so I suppose it'll keep for another few weeks.' She grew thoughtful. 'You want to wait until the end of the Season, I dare say. I can see it makes sense, you might as well enjoy all the entertainments before you finally get leg-shackled.' She cackled. 'Thank goodness it's Lizzie shackling you, she's the only one I'd trust to do it properly. You may look quiet on the surface, my boy, but still waters run deep and there's not another woman could keep you interested, and so I've been telling your mother for as long as I can remember. You have your courtship if you want it. Say no to biscuits and squeeze yourself into waistcoats that are way too small for you and play the courting game, you'll enjoy it, and so will she. You're only young once. Go wild!'

Alex took another sip of tea. His grandmother had no idea how wild he was going to be!

Chapter Six

'Stand up,' Lizzie said.

Alex grumbled, but he stood up.

'And turn round.'

'Now I know how a heifer feels when it's at the market,' he said, but he did what she told him to all the same.

'Not like that,' said Lizzie, casting her eyes heavenward as he spun on his heel. 'Slowly. We need to see what sort of clothes you should be wearing so we can decide on your new wardrobe.'

'What's wrong with what I've got on? The coat was cut by Weston, for goodness sake! He's the best tailor there is. I can't get any better than this.'

'Of course you can, your clothes may be well cut but they're not careless enough. They have to mould themselves to your body and look like a second skin. But at the same time they have to look as though you've thrown on the first thing you laid your hands on.'

'I'll never get the hang of this.'

'Of course you will, that's what we're here for, we're here to help.'

'I thought you were here to bully me and coax me and generally make my life miserable,' he complained.

'If you don't want to change . . .' remarked Lizzie.

'Oh, very well,' he sighed. 'I've started, so I may as well go through with it. So tell me, what should I do about my clothes?'

'I've got an aunt — ' said Jane.

They looked at her, startled.

'So have I,' said Lizzie.

'Me too,' said Sophy with a giggle.

'If it comes to that, so have I,' said Alex.

'Give me a chance!' laughed Jane. 'I've got an aunt who's got a cousin who's got a friend who's got a son who's a friend of Brummell's — '

'Beau Brummell's?' asked Sophy. 'The best dressed man in England?'

'What other Brummell is there? Yes, of course Beau Brummell,' said Jane, looking despairingly at Sophy, who could be very dense at times.

'And?' said Lizzie.

'And I could ask him, through my aunt's cousin's friend, for a few tips. We might even be able to arrange a meeting, and Brummell could give you some advice himself,' she said to Alex

'No, that wouldn't be any good,' said Lizzie. 'Brummell's a dandy. His clothes are always immaculate, but that's not what we want. We're not turning Alex into a dandy . . . ' She laughed, then bit her bottom lip and went on. 'We're not turning him into a dandy, we're turning him into a rake. Brummell's no use to us but Weston is. He already makes your coats, Alex, so get him to make you some new clothes that are a really tight fit. Cream breeches,' she said, narrowing her eyes to look at him more closely, 'a black coat — '

'I like blue!'

'It's not piratical enough.' She surveyed him thoughtfully. 'A satin waist coat would look nice and it wants to be embroidered. Yes, embroidered, but carelessly.'

'How do you mean, carelessly?' he said suspiciously.

'Leave that to us. It has to look sumptuous, but at the same time casual, as though it's a complete accident that it's embroidered with a gold thread that just happens to bring out the gold sparkles in your eyes.'

Alex was stunned. So were Jane and Sophy.

'What are you talking about, gold sparkles?' asked Jane.

'You must have seen them,' said Lizzie.

'No,' said Jane.

'Me neither,' said Sophy.

Even Alex hadn't seen them.

'Look in the mirror.' She steered him over to the looking glass and pointed them out. 'You can see them in strong sunlight, or candlelight, but you need to be wearing something gold in daylight to really make them shine.'

'I'd never noticed that,' said Sophy curiously, unfolding herself from the chaise longue and peering into his eyes, 'you're right.'

'You can't have been looking very hard then,' said Lizzie. 'They've always been there.'

'It's just a shame you haven't got a scar,' said Jane. 'Sparkly gold eyes are all very well, but there's something about a man with a scar.'

'Don't go putting ideas into his head,' said Lizzie reprovingly. 'You don't need a scar,' she said, turning to Alex. 'You'll do very well without one.'

'So I don't need to call someone out in the hope

they'll oblige me in a duel?' he joked.

'It's not a laughing matter,' said Lizzie. 'Doing without Anatole's puddings is one thing, risking life and limb's quite another. So we've sorted out your hair and your clothes, at least in theory — '

'Which is enough for one day,' said Alex.

Lizzie was about to protest when she changed her mind. 'You're right, a bit at a time's the best way to do it, otherwise you'll only get confused. So you'll go to Weston's tomorrow — '

'I'll be lucky if I can get to see him by the end of next week.'

'Well, do your best. Meanwhile, the three of us will sort out the waistcoat then we'll all meet back here on the 15th. And then,' she said mysteriously, 'we'll put the second part of the plan into action.'

'The second part?' asked Alex, going pale. 'I'm having difficulty handing the first part, I don't think I can take the second part.'

'Don't worry about it. All you have to worry about for the moment is going riding and fencing every day, getting rid of Anatole — '

'I'm not getting rid of him permanently, that's too much to bear. I've decided to send him on holiday instead so that he can go back to France and see all his relatives. He hasn't seen his family for ages, not since the Peace of Amiens broke down, and that's getting on for fifteen years ago, and once he's seen them he can come back again. By the time he returns, I'll either have married Arabella or I'll have made a hash of winning her. Either way I can eat what I like again.'

'Very well. Now, don't forget to cut out wine and

port —'

'You didn't say anything about wine and port,' he protested. 'And besides, rakes are always drunkards, everyone knows that.'

'But you want to get lean and mean in record time, which means you'll have to do without it. And last, but not least, don't forget to let your hair grow,' she finished.

'I think I'll go now, before you think of anything else.' He picked up his hat and walked out of the room.

'Well, we've begun,' said Lizzie to the girls, as she threw herself onto the sofa. 'I'd never realized it would be so much work, I'm exhausted.'

'It'll be worth it, though,' said Sophy, 'I can't wait to see what he looks like when we've finished with him.'

'And it's fun,' said Jane.

'Do you know?' said Lizzie, 'I rather think it is. Look out Wrexham, your crown's about to be taken. Alex's on the warpath and before long he's going to be top dog.'

'Or top rake!' said Sophy.

'Here's the waistcoat,' said Lizzie, holding it up as Alex walked into the room three weeks later. 'We've been working on it night and day. It's a good thing the season proper hasn't started or else we wouldn't have had time to do it, but we haven't had any engagements recently so we've been able to get on with it.'

'It's lucky you had a waistcoat you weren't too fond of so we could embroider over it,' said Jane. 'All we had to do was make the decorated front, otherwise it would have taken forever, as well as looking home made, which isn't what we wanted at all.'

'Isn't it a bit flamboyant?' asked Alex as he held it up in front of him. The silk front with sumptuous gold embroidery was a lot more noticeable than anything he would usually wear and he wasn't at all sure that he liked it.

'That's the point,' said Lizzie. 'It's meant to get you noticed.'

'Won't I look, well — '

'No,' said Lizzie, knowing exactly what he was going to say. 'Rakes always wear larger-than-life clothes and they never look like sissies, it's all in the way they wear them. Don't worry, you'll get the hang of it.'

'Try it on,' said Sophy, 'I want to see how it looks.'

'Me too,' said Jane.

Alex took off his coat and folded it carefully before putting it neatly over the arm of the sofa. The girls looked at each other and sighed. They really had their work cut out for them. Alex put on the waistcoat and fastened it then turned to the girls to get their opinion.

'You've lost weight,' said Lizzie 'I didn't notice when you came in, you can't really see it yet, but your waistcoat's getting too big, which proves you're getting thinner.'

She walked round him.

'It needs taking in at the back, but there's no point altering it yet because you're going to get thinner still before you wear it. Have you been going riding?'

'Twice a day,' said Alex. 'And I've been giving up on my food, though it hasn't been easy. My mother keeps asking me what's wrong with me and my grandmother's convinced I'm trying to impress you.'

'Me?' Lizzie was startled. 'Whatever would you want to impress me for? My feelings for you aren't going to change just because you stride around looking long and lean and casting mocking glances in every direction.'

'Mocking glances?' Alex looked nervous. 'You never said anything about mocking glances. This is getting harder by the minute.'

'Don't worry,' Lizzie reassured him. 'That will come later, but for now, the waistcoat hits the right note. It'll get you noticed but at the same time, as long as you wear it carelessly enough it won't look sissy.'

Alex took it off and put it neatly over the chair, then picked up his coat.

'No, don't put it on again,' said Lizzie as he was going to do it.

Alex paused.

'You need to learn how to take it off properly.'

He looked at her open-mouthed. 'You don't mean to tell me there's a special way to take my coat off.'

'Oh, yes we do,' said Sophy.

'I don't believe you, you're making fun of me,' he said, looking from one to the other of them.

'No, we're not,' said Jane. 'You can't take your coat off so carefully.'

'And then fold it neatly,' giggled Sophy.

'Before putting it over the arm of the sofa,' said Jane.

'What's wrong with that? I haven't got my valet with me and you can't expect me to ring for the butler over something as trifling as this.'

'Heaven forbid!' said Lizzie. 'Rakes never have valets, and their butlers are there to let women of ill repute into their bachelor apartments late at night, not to help them off with their coats.'

'Then what do you expect me to do?'

'You need to tear it off. And don't stand still whilst you do it, rakes never stand still. Stride across the room.'

'For heaven's sake!'

'Why, can't you do two things at once?' asked Sophy.

'Alex was the champion head-patter-and-stomach-rubber in our neck of the woods for many years,' Lizzie defended him.

'Just what he needs to do if he wants to be a rake!' said Sophy mischievously.

'Try it,' Jane said to Alex.

'Oh, very well, but I'll have to put it on again first.'

He slipped into his coat and then took it off whilst walking across the room.

'Better,' said Lizzie encouragingly, 'but you need to stride, and don't take it off so small-ly.'

'Small-lly?' he asked in astonishment. 'Is that a word?'

'It is now. Use bigger movements, wave your arms about more - that's right,' she said, her heart sinking as Alex began flailing like a windmill. 'Only not quite as much as that. Then throw your coat on the floor.'

'But it'll get filthy!'

'You can't worry about that now, fling it down any old how . . . carelessly.'

Alex glared mutinously, but he flung his coat down on the floor. 'Though I don't know why I'm bothering, no-one's going to see me taking my coat off.'

'I thought Arabella was. I thought that was the whole point,' said Jane naughtily.

Lizzie was stricken. For a minute she didn't like the thought of Alex taking off his coat for Arabella. Then she told herself not to be so stuffy, helping Alex win Arabella was the whole point of doing it.

'It seems to me rakes spend most of their time being careless,' he said with a frown. 'Though I can't for the life of me think why.'

'It's half the attraction,' said Jane. 'They don't seem to try too hard, they never care about anything.'

'But if they don't care about anything they won't care about the women in their life,' said Alex.

'That's the point,' sighed Sophy with a long-suffering air.

'You mean you want someone who isn't going to care about you?' asked Alex in astonishment. He picked up his coat and put it on. 'What's the point of that?'

Sophy shrugged. 'I don't know. I suppose it's because then we won't have to care about them so that if they ask us to marry them - which isn't very likely, I'll admit, because rakes don't generally do that sort of thing - but if they do then we don't have to worry about hurting their feelings because they haven't got any. It's awfully difficult you know, having to turn men down. It's not nice to have to hurt them.'

'You have a point,' said Jane, looking admiringly at Sophy. 'That's one of the big attractions. We like rakes because we don't have to worry about hurting them, so we can be ourselves - which is another point. We can be ourselves. Not just without worrying about hurting them, but without worrying about shocking them either. They don't care about convention so they won't be outraged if we say that side saddles are ridiculous. They won't mind if we say we're much happier riding astride, which we always do when we're on our own on our estates — '

'I thought Lizzie was the only one who did that,' said Alex.

'No, we're all guilty of it,' said Sophy. 'But there you are, you see, we have to feel guilty about it, and why? We like riding astride. We don't like having to sit on side saddles. And there you are, you see, I can say that sort of thing to a rake and he'll laugh and like me the better for it but if I say it to a gentleman he'll go all stiff and quiet and say, "Quite so" down his nose, as though I've just said something terrible but he's too much of a gentleman to point it out.'

'You can say it to me and I'm not a rake. You've just done it.'

'That's different. You're Alex. We've grown up with you. But we couldn't say it to anyone we didn't know, and not to half the people we do know, either.'

'They'd think we were fast, or hoydens, or fit only for the demi monde,' giggled Sophy.

'So when I'm a rake women will say that sort of thing to me?' he asked curiously.

'Of course. But you mustn't agree.'

'Why not?'

'They don't. Rakes, I mean. They just laugh sardonically, or give a mocking smile, or look smouldering, but they never agree.'

'Well if that's all they do I should have it off pat in no time. I thought it was going to be difficult, but as long as I'm careless and laugh — '

'Sardonically,' put in Jane.

'And laugh sardonically every time a woman opens her mouth, it'll be easy.'

Lizzie said, 'You're getting the hang of it. Now let's return to business. The point of this meeting is to sort out your clothes, have you seen Weston yet?'

'Yes.'

'And?'

'He's promised my coat'll be so tight I'll have to be prised into it with a shoe horn and I'll have to be lowered into my breeches with a winch!'

Lizzie put her hands on her hips. 'You're not taking this seriously,' she said accusingly.

'I am, I promise,' he said with a laugh. 'So, I've seen Weston and arranged for a tight coat and breeches,' he said, ticking it off on his fingers, 'and you've given me a waistcoat, so all I need now's a shirt, a cravat — '

'Those are easy,' said Lizzie. 'A rake's shirt and cravat are like anyone else's.'

' — and a pair of boots.'

'Hessians. But dusty,' said Lizzie.

'What? Not polished?'

'No. A rake always looks like he's been somewhere exciting, and he can't do that if his boots are too clean.'

'Very well,' sighed Alex. 'Dusty boots.'

'Good. Well, I think that's about it for today,' said Lizzie. 'Now it's time for us to tell you our plan.'

Alex sat down. 'What plan?' He looked at her suspiciously.

'To get you up to scratch. Sophy's got a cousin in Kent and we're all going to stay with her so that you can get some practise on diamonds of the first water before you have to commit yourself in public - well, in London, which amounts to the same thing. No one really cares what happens in the provinces, in fact they'll never know, so if you make an absolute fool of yourself it won't matter. Then when you've got it down to a fine art, you can come back to town and capture Arabella's heart. Besides, it will give you a few extra weeks to trim down.'

'I don't think I'm going to find any diamonds of the first water in Kent,' he remarked.

'Maybe that's a bit of an exaggeration, but they'll be the belles of their neighbourhood, so they'll react to you in the same way. They'll think they're too good for you and you'll have to fascinate them and make them come running. It'll be good practise.'

'And if it doesn't work you won't have lost anything — '

'Such as?' asked Alex.

'Your pride,' giggled Sophy.

'Your self-respect,' Jane teased.

'I lost that long ago, the day I met the three of you,' he joked. 'But I see your point. I can cut my teeth on the beauties of Kent and then come back to London and sweep Arabella off her feet.'

'That's the spirit,' said Jane.

'You'll have her eating out of your hand in no time,' said Sophy.

But rather to his surprise, Lizzie didn't say anything.

Chapter Seven

'So this is Kent,' said Alex a week later. He helped Lizzie out of the carriage on the turning circle of the grand country house belonging to Sophy's aunt. Lizzie, Jane and Sophy were going to be staying with Sophy's aunt whilst they were in Kent.

'Yes. I'm sure you'll like it. There'll be lots of local jamborees, plenty of entertainments for you to cut your teeth on before we go back to London.'

'I'm looking forward to it,' said Alex.

'Now you're sure you'll be all right at the inn?' Lizzie said, looking at him questioningly. 'Sophy would have asked her aunt to put you up here as well, but if she'd done that then everyone would have known who you were. And if everyone had known you were a friend of Sophy's, you wouldn't have been able to convince them all you were a wild rake.'

'I prefer staying at The King's Head,' said Alex. 'I don't think I could smile mockingly at all the local débutantes if I'd been playing a hand of cribbage with my hosts in a civilised fashion half an hour before.'

'No, it would be rather difficult. There are no entertainments until next week so I suggest you use the time for long walks and riding. You can even go swimming if the weather's warm enough. Mind you don't eat too much, and remember to go without wine and port. That way you'll be at your leanest before the first entertainment comes around.'

'I'll look like a greyhound,' he teased her.

'Good. Sophy and I will come and see you on

Friday afternoon. We'll sneak into your private sitting-room when the maids are not about, and then we can help you get ready for the ball at the Assembly Rooms on Friday night.'

'I'll see you on Friday then,' said Alex,

He got back in the carriage and it rumbled off to The King's Head.

Lizzie turned round and, went up the imposing stone steps to the house, followed by her maid. Sophy's aunt lived in a Jacobean residence. It was a large, symmetrical building with an imposing façade, but inside it was more homely.

'Oh, my dear, there you are. How was your journey?' asked Sophy's aunt as she met Lizzie hospitably in the hall. 'The roads are dreadful at this time of year. All those pot holes! But you seem to have made it in one piece. Come in.'

They went through into the drawing-room where Sophy was sitting in front of the blazing fire.

'So there you are at last! I thought you'd never get here. You've met my aunt, but this is Uncle Horace and my cousin James.'

Uncle Horace prised himself out of his chair next to the fire and said: 'How do you do, m'dear?' whilst James, a merry young man with dancing eyes, bowed over her hand.

Once they'd all said 'hello' they settled down to some splendid refreshments, which were made up of seed cake and sandwiches with plenty of hot tea.

'We are so pleased to have you here,' said Sophy's aunt. 'It will make such a change from being in town. I know everyone thinks London is wonderful but it can be terribly dull at this time of year.'

'Dreadful place,' put in Sophy's uncle.

Lizzie caught Sophy's eye and smiled. Uncle Horace had never liked London. He thought it was noisy and dusty and far too crowded.

'Have another sandwich, Miss Carstairs,' said James. 'You must be hungry after your journey, and dinner won't be for another couple of hours.'

'Thank you, I will,' said Lizzie.

'I wasn't at all surprised when Sophy said you wanted to spend some time in the country,' went on Sophy's aunt. 'I don't blame you for wanting to avoid the measles.'

Lizzie looked at Sophy in surprise. Sophy looked uncomfortable, but Lizzie guessed that Sophy had wanted an excuse for the visit, so she must have told her aunt there had been an outbreak of measles in the capital. Lizzie felt a bit guilty, and she could tell by Sophy's expression that she felt a bit guilty, too, but she consoled herself by thinking that the excuse didn't hurt anyone, and it was all in a good cause. If it helped them turn Alex turn into a magnet for wonderful women then it would have been worth it - something even Sophy's aunt would agree with, if she ever discovered the truth.

'It would never do to be covered in spots when the Season proper starts,' went on Sophy's aunt. 'And besides, some country air will do you good. London's too full of chimneys, to my way of thinking. All that coal dust in the air isn't good for the lungs, and it isn't as though you will be bored. There is always plenty to do here, as long as it doesn't rain. We seem to have had a dry spell recently, thank goodness, and the sun has been nice and warm for the time of year.'

'In other words, you will enjoy Kent more than London,' James teased.

They all laughed. Mr and Mrs Lyndhurst's' partiality for their home county was plain to see.

'I thought Jane would have got here before me,' said Lizzie as James offered her another cucumber sandwich. She wondered when the third of the girls was going to arrive.

'She should have been here in time for lunch, she was going to set off early this morning, ' said Sophy. She glanced at the clock. It was a sweet little thing made out of ormolu and the hands said it was almost three.

'It's nothing to worry about,' said James. 'You know what the roads are like. With all the potholes and wheel ruts, they are in a disgraceful state. It's a wonder anyone can get anywhere at all.'

'Oh, well, as long as she's here in time for dinner,' said Sophy's aunt. 'And now, Sophy, take Lizzie upstairs and show her to her room. I expect she'll want to rest after her journey. We will see you both again at five o'clock.'

Lizzie and Sophy left the room. They climbed the imposing oak-panelled staircase a little way before taking the right hand fork as it split in two and then went along the landing to the bedrooms.

'You're in the room next to me and Jane's on the other side,' said Sophy as she showed Lizzie into a pretty room with a four poster bed and red frilly curtains at the window. 'There are interconnecting doors in between the rooms so it'll be easy to talk things over without Aunt Cecelia knowing anything about it.'

'I'm glad you didn't tell her,' said Lizzie. 'It would have made Alex very embarrassed if anyone else knew what was going on, and the last thing he wants is to be embarrassed. He wants to get his confidence whilst he's down here so that he can stride into a London ballroom and sweep Arabella off her feet.' She gave Sophy a humorous glance. 'But even so . . . measles?'

Sophy pulled a face. 'It was the best thing I could think of. Aunt Cecelia didn't want to know why we wanted to leave London, to her way of thinking, wanting to leave London and visit Kent is only common sense, but James scented something and kept asking what had brought me down here, and that set Uncle Horace to wondering whether there was any reason for it, too. In the end, to keep James quiet, I invented an outbreak of measles.' She looked thoughtful. 'I still thinks he suspects something, though. We'll have to be careful, and not talk about Alex when he's around.'

Lizzie nodded. 'It would be awful if he discovered the truth. It's very important he doesn't know who Alex is. In fact it's very important nobody knows, because if they discover he's our friend they'll never believe he's a rake. Besides, he needs to have an air of mystery about him, and he can't have that if everyone knows who he is.'

Sophy agreed. 'As soon as Jane arrives, we must warn her not to say anything.'

'That sounds like her now,' said Lizzie, as the sound of carriage wheels crunching on gravel drifted up to the bedroom. She went over to the window and pulled back the curtains. Sure enough, a carriage had just pulled up in front of the house. Sophy joined her at the window. The carriage door opened and Jane climbed out.

'At last,' said Sophy, 'Now we're all here the fun can begin.'

Chapter Eight

Lizzie was enjoying her time in Kent. Sophy's aunt and uncle were hospitable people, and made Lizzie and Jane feel very welcome. As Sophy's aunt had said, there was plenty to do, and they passed the days until Friday by exploring the neighbourhood. Sophy was a good guide, and before long they knew their way to the best milliner's, draper's and dressmaker's for miles around.

The one difficulty was James. He often went with them on their visits to the neighbouring town, or on their walks, and they knew they would have to put him off when they wanted to visit Alex at The King's Head. They were lucky, though. James, too, was going to the Assembly Rooms ball, and on the Friday afternoon he had to visit his tailor to pick up his new coat. It meant they were able to go to The King's Head without having to tell him he couldn't go out with them, which would make him curious.

They arrived at The King's Head shortly after lunch. It was a half-timbered building and it had once been a prosperous coaching inn. Now it was a simple hostelry that had good food and comfortable accommodation for anyone who wanted to stay in the area, as well as having a tap room for the locals to drink in.

The girls waited downstairs until they were sure there was no one about, then they slipped up to his private sitting room. They had no trouble finding it, because Alex had taken the only private suite at the inn, and Sophy knew her way around, having visited the inn on many occasions when other friends and family members had been staying there. Her parents were very hospitable, but they did not always have enough guest rooms when there were big family gatherings, and besides, the young men of the family often preferred to stay at the inn. It gave them more freedom to come and go, and they could pursue their amorous adventures without anyone seeing them.

They knocked at the door and Alex opened it.

They stood and stared. He was looking completely different. All the weeks of going without rich food, and spending more time riding, fencing and visiting Gentleman Jackson's gym, had finally paid off, getting rid of his chubby body and turning it into something long and sleek His hair had grown out of its usual short style and it was almost touching his collar. He really looked very rakish, and for a minute Lizzie felt rather shocked. But then his face lit up on seeing them, and Lizzie gave a sigh of relief because this was the Alex she knew.

'I thought you'd never get here. I've been waiting for you for ages.' He glanced down the corridor to make sure no maids were about. 'Come in.'

The sitting room was a bit shabby, but it was clean and the furniture looked comfortable. There was a big sofa opposite the fireplace, and there were two horsehair-stuffed chairs on either side of it. There was a window with small panes of glass in it, looking out over the road.

'Are you all set for tonight?' asked Sophy.

He nodded.

'Have your clothes arrived from London?' asked

Lizzie. 'I know you said your valet would bring them here as soon as they were ready, but I still think you should have gone yourself.'

'No need,' said Alex. 'They got here this morning. I had to pay Weston a fortune to get them ready for today because everyone wants him making their clothes, but he came up trumps. They're hanging up in the dressing room.'

'Go and put them on,' said Lizzie, sitting down on the sofa. 'We want to see how you're going to look tonight.'

Alex went through into the dressing-room. Ten minutes later he came out in his skin-tight coat and breeches. His shirt and cravat were new so they were very white and they looked really rather nice next to his skin, which had been turned light brown by the unseasonably warm sunshine they'd been enjoying ever since they'd arrived.

'Well?' he asked.

Lizzie was speechless. It was most disturbing seeing Alex dressed up like that. It made him seem different. But he was still the same Alex. How odd. And how strangely perturbing.

'Well!' gasped Sophy, finally able to speak.

Not only had the weeks with plenty of exercise and none of Anatole's cooking trimmed him down, giving him a sleeker, leaner look, but his long dark hair showed off the fine cut of his cheekbones, which were revealed in all their glory now that his face had lost most of its spare fat. His clothes were clinging to him like a mariner clinging to a shipwreck and they showed off his new lean form, with muscles Lizzie had never seen before showing underneath them.

'You don't like it,' he said with a grimace. 'I knew it wouldn't work.'

'We like it,' said Lizzie firmly. 'We're just speechless, that's all, you look so different, so — '

'Desirable,' said Sophy dreamily.

'Really?' Alex's eyebrows raised and then his face broke into a grin.

'Really,' said Jane, looking her approval.

'It's a transformation,' said Lizzie. 'You'll draw women's eyes everywhere you go, that's a certainty. There won't be a woman who can keep her eyes off you at the ball, they'll all be swooning over you.'

He looked delighted, then his face fell. 'That's all very well to begin with, but it won't get me very far,' he said, sounding worried. 'It's one thing to look like a rake but I'm going to have to act like one as well, and I don't know what to do.'

The three girls looked at each other. What Alex said was true. Looking like a rake was one thing, acting like one was quite another.

Lizzie collected her thoughts and said, 'Very well, it's time to begin. We might as well start at the beginning. The first thing you need to know is how to make an entrance. It's no use walking into the ballroom in the usual way.'

She thought of her earlier advice to him, when she'd told him to walk like a panther, and she shuddered. That definitely hadn't worked out as planned! This time she decided not to mention jungle animals.

She said, 'You have to do it cynically, as though you don't really want to be there and you know you're going to be bored. But you've decided to come anyway because you haven't got anything better to do for half an hour, before you go off on an exciting adventure.'

'I don't know about that,' said Alex with a frown. 'It seems rude to me.'

Lizzie sighed. 'That's the whole point, rakes are rude. Otherwise they wouldn't be rakes, they'd be gentlemen. You're going to need some practise so you can do it perfectly tonight. Now, give it a try.'

After a few grumbles Alex went back into the bedroom and closed the door. Then he opened it again and walked into the sitting-room. As he did so he heaved a heavy sigh.

'What are you sighing for?' asked Lizzie in surprise. Really, Alex did the most peculiar things.

'I'm showing I don't want to be there.'

Sophy spluttered with merriment.

'Not like that!' said Jane. 'You'll be a laughing stock if you do something like that!'

'Here,' said Sophy. 'Like this.' She went out of the room and came in again, doing a fair impression of Wrexham's careless walk.

Alex looked at her in amazement.

'Go on,' said Lizzie pushing him towards the door again. 'You can do it. It's just like playing charades. You were always very good at charades. All you have to do is copy Jane and you'll do it to perfection.'

Brightening at the thought that it was just like charades, Alex tried again and walked into the room in a very rake-like fashion.

'Very good,' said Sophy, clapping her hands.

Alex's face broke into a grin and he gave a bow.

'It's easy once you know how,' he said. Then he became serious again, 'All right, I know how to walk into the ballroom, but what do I do then?'

'You find something to lean against,' said Lizzie.

'Negligently,' added Jane.

Sophy demonstrated, leaning against the wall whilst looking round mockingly with a superior smile on her face.

Alex had always been quick to learn things, so he copied her and he managed to do it very well.

'You're coming on,' said Lizzie admiringly. 'Now, suppose a young lady approaches you. I'll be her.' She stood up and walked coquettishly over to him, batting her eyelids for all she was worth.

He looked taken aback for a minute but then he recovered himself and said, 'How do you do?'

'No, no, no,' she said in exasperation. 'Rakes never say how do you do.'

'Then what do they say?'

'They don't say anything. They just look at people.'

'Like this?' He stared at her.

'No, not like that!'

'Then how?'

'Give a mocking smile,' said Sophy.

Alex had been practising mocking smiles in front of the mirror and had got it off to a fine art, so he had no trouble in doing it - much to Lizzie's surprise. Her eyes opened wide.

'That's very good,' she said. She felt suddenly uncomfortable, although she couldn't think why. Alex had done just what she'd told him to do, and had done it well. Perhaps too well. But that was nonsense, because how could he do it too well? She gathered her thoughts and returned them to what she was doing. 'The next thing to do is to look the young lady up and down,' she said.

'All right. I can manage that.'

'No!' She laughed as his eyes ran over her. 'Not like that. You look like you're buying a horse! Any minute now you'll be pulling back my lips and looking at my teeth!'

The girls giggled, and even Alex had to laugh.

'Well how then?' he asked.

'You have to look at her as though you're undressing her with your eyes.'

He blushed, and the girls laughed again.

Then Lizzie became serious. 'You've got to be able to do it,' she said firmly. 'It's one of the things rakes always do. Now try again.'

'Not on your life. I'm not making a fool of myself in front of all of you. I'll practise on my own, when the three of you have gone back to Sophy's aunt's.'

'Oh, very well,' said Lizzie.

'Then what? Tell me what I ought to do next.'

'Then you kiss her hand - slowly.'

'How on earth do I kiss her hand slowly?'

'First of all you lift it halfway to your lips, just touching her fingertips with your own. Then you look deep into her eyes. Then you give a mocking smile. Then you kiss her hand, and all the time you never take your eyes away from her, then you lower it slowly down to her side. And all the time you keep looking her in the eye, so that she's held to you by the magnetism of your gaze.'

'I'll never remember all that,' he groaned.

'You will. Just have a try.'

He lifted her hand by the fingertips and carried it halfway to his lips. Then his eyes looked into her own and he gave her a mocking smile before brushing the back of her hand with his lips.

Lizzie felt a sudden rush of gooseflesh wash over her. Goodness, how odd! She hadn't expected that. It felt most peculiar. She hoped she wasn't going down with something. The last thing she wanted was to be in bed with a chill when there was so much to be done.

Then he lowered her hand to her side.

'Well?' he asked. 'How did I do?'

Lizzie was still feeling strange. She must remember to have a hot toddy when she got back to Sophy's aunt's house in order to ward off any coughs and colds. She couldn't afford to be confined to her sick room, not know, when Alex needed her help.

She stirred herself. 'Good,' she murmured. 'Yes, it was very good.'

'But I think you'd better practise again,' said Sophy.

She stood up and held her hand out to him.

He laughed and then he did it again, this time kissing her hand.

Jane stood up. 'Me too,' she said.

'Whoever would have thought it?' said Sophy as the three girls left the inn, once they had done all they could to help Alex for the time being. 'It felt lovely when Alex kissed my hand.'

'Mmm. I almost forgot it was Alex,' said Jane as the three girls walked back to Sophy's aunt's house.

'We'll make a rake of him yet.' She turned to Lizzie. 'You're very quiet, Lizzie.'

Lizzie, who was still feeling a little bit peculiar but didn't like to say anything in case it worried the girls, said: 'One of us has to be. You and Sophy have been rattling away for the last ten minutes. I haven't been able to get a word in edgeways!'

Now where have they been? wondered James, as he saw the three girls returning to the house. There's something about them, as though they've been up to mischief. I wonder why they left London to come down to Kent in the middle of the Little Season? That faradiddle about the measles might have fooled my mother, but it won't fool me. Sophy's up to something. I wonder what it is?

As he looked out of the window his eyes fell on Jane. She'd grown up since the last time he'd seen her, and she was looking really rather beautiful. He liked the way there were little wisps of hair escaping from her bun at the back, and he loved the way they curled into the nape of her neck, like a kitten curling up in its basket. They looked just as soft and downy as a kitten, and they made him want to stroke them. He was cross with himself for having such unsuitable feelings. Jane was Sophy's friend, and he wasn't going to compromise his cousin's companion.

The three girls passed out of his sight, but he couldn't help thinking that Jane had grown into a beauty. It was a pity he was too young to settle down.

Because a man might like to marry a girl like that.

Chapter Nine

Back at The King's Head, Alex was practising his sardonic laughter in front of the mirror. He had had a few tries, and some of them had been quite good, but then they had gradually become worse until they'd become inane grins. He gave a sigh. He thought he'd mastered the art, but it had gone again. It was all right when he concentrated. If he imagined himself playing the part of a wicked squire in a charade, or one of the amateur theatricals he and Lizzie had indulged in as children - and still indulged in, if truth be told, on long winter evenings when there wasn't much else to do - he made a decent job of it. But if he lost his concentration he looked more like someone who'd trapped his foot in a door, instead of a wildly handsome rake.

Never mind, he'd managed a number of mocking smiles, a few cynical laughs and a three or four dark scowls since the girls had left, so it might be better if he gave it a rest. That way he'd be fresh for the evening, when he would be putting his new powers to the test. But before he left it entirely, there was just one more thing he wanted to try, and that was undressing a young lady with his eyes.

It had made him blush at first when Lizzie had mentioned it, but then he'd recalled Wrexham giving a number of ladies the once over and now he knew what the rake had been doing. Anything Wrexham could do . . . He tried it in the mirror, but unfortunately, because he had no desire to undress himself, all he did was go cross-eyed.

I need to think about Arabella, he thought. Now there's someone I definitely want to undress with my eyes. But to his surprise he didn't see Arabella, he saw Lizzie instead.

How peculiar, he thought, but then he realized it must have been because he'd been practising on her that afternoon. An image of Lizzie was no good, though, because he didn't want to undress Lizzie with his eyes, and anyway he didn't need to. He'd seen her in her chemise on any number of occasions. They'd gone swimming together a lot when they had been children, and she had always stripped her dress off so that it wouldn't get spoiled.

He found himself smiling at the memory. No one had known about their swimming escapades, of course. It wasn't the done thing for a young lady to go swimming in the sea, and it was even worse for her to go swimming with a member of the opposite sex, even if he was just the neighbour's son. They would have been in dreadful trouble if anyone had found out, but fortunately no one ever had.

Lizzie had always been a bit of a tomboy when she'd been a little girl. Her mother had always been trying to stop her doing unsuitable things, such as going swimming or climbing trees. Poor Mrs Carstairs! She'd put endless energy into trying to teach Lizzie how to do ladylike things like painting watercolours or embroidering fire screens, but it had been hopeless. Lizzie had always been an outdoor girl and she had never liked sitting indoors on a fine day, whatever she was expected to do.

He laughed as he remembered that Mrs Carstairs

had taken Lizzie outside to paint in despair, thinking that if Lizzie must always be outside then she could learn to paint landscapes, but it hadn't made things any better. Lizzie had always been active girl. She wanted to be outside and doing things, not sitting still, and she had knocked over the water jar and then dropped her painting face down so it was ruined.

But this wasn't getting him anywhere. He wasn't meant to be thinking of Lizzie, he was meant to be thinking of Arabella. Now if he could just get rid of the image of Lizzie from his thoughts and remind himself that he already knew what she looked like in her chemise - although she'd filled out a bit since those days and she had also changed her shape, he thought, as he remembered the way she'd looked in her latest ball gown, with its puffed sleeves showing off her shapely arms and its low neck showing off . . . But he was doing it again, thinking about Lizzie when he was meant to be thinking about Arabella.

He made himself concentrate and an image of Arabella floated before his eyes. It started to take shape slowly as he concentrated harder. First of all came her white bosom, followed by her trim waist and her curved hips, then her long legs and, last of all, her tiny feet. He let his eyes roam all over her imaginary body as he pictured what she'd look like without anything on and he was surprised to see that his gaze was distinctly heated when he caught sight of himself in the mirror. Now if he could only get the same kind of heat in his eyes at the Assembly Rooms ball, he'd be well on his way to being a rake!

But that was enough for now. Being a rake was fun, but it was also hard work and he needed a rest.

Besides, his clothes were beginning to cut off his blood supply, and he wanted to get out of them.

Stripping off his new coat and breeches before they could do him any permanent damage, he changed into his comfortable old coat and breeches. Ah! what a relief. They were particularly roomy now that he'd lost so much weight, and felt wonderful.

He looked out of the window to see what the weather was like, and it was still fine. He'd just have time for a ride before having an early dinner. After that, it would be time to go to the Assembly Rooms and try out his new-found powers on the lovely young ladies of Kent.

Chapter Ten

'What time did he say he was arriving?' asked Jane as the three girls stood in the ballroom of the Assembly Rooms, eagerly waiting for Alex to arrive.

'Ten o'clock,' said Lizzie.

'That doesn't give him much time to make an impression,' said Sophy with a frown. 'We keep early hours in the country and the ball will be over and done with by eleven. Mr Dickinson's the Master of Ceremonies, and he doesn't like late nights because he has to get home to his elderly mother in time to help her to bed.'

'That's the whole point,' said Lizzie. 'It will leave all the young ladies who see him here tonight wanting more. It's no use getting him to arrive at eight o'clock so that everyone is bored with him before the evening's over. Besides, it will mean there is less time for anything to go wrong.'

'And it will help him to make an entrance,' said Jane. 'He will be more noticeable if he arrives later on rather than with everyone else.'

'Miss Fearnley, may I have the honour of your hand for the next dance?' asked James, who had just joined them and who was looking remarkably smart in his new blue tailcoat and a pair of knee breeches.

Jane dropped him a curtsey. 'Thank you, you may.'

Lizzie was claimed by Marcus Lemming, a local landowner, and Sophy's hand was sought by Lord Marlsbury. They all joined Jane and James on the dance floor.

The Assembly Rooms were rather shabby but they were nice and big. There was room for twenty couples to stand up together in the long oak-panelled room, with the ladies taking their place down one side and the gentlemen facing them down the other, ready for the first country dance.

The orchestra was made up of fiddles which were played by the local blacksmith and the village butcher, and some more tradesmen who were trying to learn the instrument. It sounded a bit odd when they started to play, but no one minded, and the gentlemen bowed to their partners, the ladies curtseyed to the gentlemen, and they all began to dance.

Jane and James, Sophy and Lord Marlsbury, Lizzie and Marcus Lemming all danced with enthusiasm, getting distinctly hot and bothered before retreating to the side of the room when the dance was over to eat ices and cool off. The rest of the evening passed in a very pleasant fashion, with the girls dancing every dance, until the clock at the far end of the Assembly Rooms began to strike. Sophy nudged Lizzie, and Lizzie looked at Jane. It was ten o'clock.

Right on cue the door opened and Alex stood there in the doorway just as the girls had taught him to do, casting a cynical glance over the proceedings. Everybody's heads turned towards him. The gentlemen immediately looked daggers at Alex, whilst the ladies began to flutter their fans. To Lizzie's amusement, two young females next to Jane looked as though they were about to swoon. Against all the odds, it was working!

She turned her attention back to Alex. He cast a contemptuous look around him, as though everyone present was beneath his notice, and then swaggered into the ballroom.

'Goodness, that swagger's excellent,' said Lizzie. 'Who taught him to do that?'

'I don't know,' said Jane. 'I think it must be one of his own ideas. I certainly didn't teach him how to do it. Did you?' she asked, turning to Sophy.

Sophy shook her head. 'Still, he said he would have a few surprises for us this evening. It looks like he was right.'

'Do you know him?' asked James.

The girls hadn't seen James as he had walked over to them, meaning to ask Jane for the next dance, and he had heard part of their conversation. He was like every other gentleman in the room, he wanted to find out who the mysterious stranger could be.

Jane was put on the spot, she didn't know what to say. She didn't like lying, especially not to James, but telling the truth would give the game away.

'I've never seen anyone who looks like that before,' she said.

It was true in a way, for whilst of course she knew Alex she had never seen him dressed up in a tight coat and satin breeches with his hair falling wildly onto his collar before. Even when he'd dressed up that afternoon he hadn't arranged his hair in such a carelessly rakish fashion.

'Neither have I,' said James. 'He looks like a loose screw to me. You girls had better keep well away from him.'

'He's probably rusticating,' said Mr Keybrook,

who had been about to ask Sophy to dance and who was now looking at Alex with obvious dislike. He didn't like having a rival for the ladies' attention, it was the last thing he wanted.

Good, thought Lizzie, who was watching them with amusement. The gentlemen have had their noses put out of joint, that's an encouraging sign.

Alex was by now leaning carelessly against a pillar and looking at everyone with a sardonic gleam in his eye, just as he'd been taught to do.

'May I have the pleasure of this dance?' James asked Jane.

Jane was very pleased he'd asked her to dance and so she said, 'Yes.'

She gave him her hand. She was starting to enjoy the evening.

Mr Keybrook asked Sophy to dance, and Sophy said, 'Yes,' so he took her out onto the floor.

A young man called Mr Owen asked Lizzie to dance, and Lizzie said, 'Yes.'

But as soon as the dance was over the girls said 'No' to any more partners, saying they were too hot to dance, because they wanted to see how Alex got on.

'What a nuisance this whole rake business is,' said Lizzie with a sigh, as she watched Alex lounging negligently against his pillar. 'If only it wasn't for Arabella then Alex would be talking to us now, and later on he would ask me for a dance.' She was missing Alex's company and she was wishing he had never started all this nonsense, even though she had to admit he looked lovely in his new clothes.

'I'm very pleased for him,' said Sophy. 'All our

hard work has been worth it. He's remembered everything we taught him, and he looks just like a rake.'

'Yes,' said Lizzie, a bit wistfully, 'he does.'

Alex, meanwhile, was having a wonderful time. He had spent the early part of the evening pacing nervously up and down his private sitting-room at The King's Head, waiting until it was time for him to leave for the ball, but as soon as he had flung open the door of the Assembly Rooms his nerves had vanished. He had started to enjoy himself, first of all because of the way the young ladies had turned to look at him, and then because of the way the gentlemen had shot him barbed glances. He thought the evening was going to be a great success.

He was buoyed up by his entrance so he moved like a panther over to a convenient pillar and he leant against it carelessly, and while he did he it cast cynical glances over everyone else. I might have come to this ball because I had nothing better to do, his attitude said, but I'm still finding it a dead bore.

He caught sight of the girls out of the corner of his eye and he could tell they'd been pleased with his entrance. Their hands had all been claimed for the next dance and he was pleased for them because they didn't like being wallflowers. Lizzie was dancing with a fish-faced young man, someone who definitely wasn't good enough for her, but he'd better give his own life his attention if he wanted to pass himself off as a rake.

His eyes roved scornfully over the room again. They fell on a pretty young lady in a white muslin gown, the sort who would not have normally given him a second glance, and sure enough, she wasn't giving him a second glance, either, but only because she hadn't been able to end the first one. Her eyes were stuck to him and she was looking at him as though she were a very hungry dog and he were a very juicy bone.

He looked away from her, but even so he could still see her out of the corner of his eye. He watched her as she walked nonchalantly over to him and dropped her fan.

'Oh!' she exclaimed, with big, wide eyes, looking straight at him. 'I appear to have dropped my fan. How clumsy of me.'

She smiled at him winningly. Her blue eyes were sparkling and her lips were as red as roses. She was almost as pretty as Arabella.

He was going to pick up the fan, like any normal young man would have done, and then give it back to her with a smile, but he stopped himself just in time. He remembered everything Lizzie had said to him and so he didn't do anything, he just stood there and ignored it.

The young lady fluttered her eyelashes and simpered at him in the sort of way he'd always wanted young ladies to flutter their eyelashes and simper at him, but when she realized he wasn't going to pick her fan up she began to look foolish, and at last she started blushing and had to pick it up herself.

Alex didn't like it much. He felt mean when he saw how embarrassed she was. It really wasn't very nice of him to have treated her in that way, even if he was a rake. He was tempted to tell her he was sorry for being rude and he was just going to do it when she gave him a look of such devoted adoration that he kept quiet instead.

She was blushing and looking decidedly awkward and she walked away from him, but she couldn't resist a last look over her shoulder. Her look showed him that not only would she be happy to dance with him if he asked her later on, which of course, being a rake, he wouldn't, but that she would probably swoon into the bargain as well.

This is like falling off a log, he thought, as another young lady looked towards him with a longing look. All I have to do is stand here and look at everyone as though they're not good enough for me and they all think I'm wonderful.

It got even easier a minute later when a second young lady walked over to him and said, 'I hope you will forgive me for speaking to you like this, when we haven't even been introduced, but I feel like I know you. Haven't we met somewhere before?'

He suddenly felt uncomfortable, because when she asked him a question he didn't know what to say. He thought quickly, but it was no use, he couldn't come up with a good answer. A real rake would have thought of a put-down, but he wasn't quite up to that yet so instead he covered the silence with a derisory laugh.

The young lady bit her bottom lip and went away, but not without giving him a lot of languishing looks before she did it. Even when she'd returned to her own party she didn't lose interest in him. She kept looking at him every few seconds when she was meant to be talking to another gentleman, which made the other gentleman very cross. It made Alex very happy, because he was usually the other gentleman and now he was the one everyone wanted to be with, not the one everyone didn't want to be with.

It wasn't only the younger ladies, he noticed, the older ones were casting him longing glances too, in fact one of them was walking towards him right now.

He couldn't believe it. She was the handsomest woman he had ever seen in his life. Her dark hair was arranged with one ringlet falling over her bare shoulder and her scarlet satin dress was cut low, wrapping itself round all her curves like a cat wrapping itself round a tree.

She was a mature beauty, she must be nearly thirty, and she was even better than the young girls, because she was all red and ripe, and she was the sort of woman who usually laughed at him or asked him to get her a glass of champagne, like he was a footman or a little boy.

By now Alex was really enjoying himself. He could hardly wait for her to reach him, though he made sure he didn't show it. He hardly looked at her, and when he did, he made sure he had a look of cynical amusement on his face.

She stopped in front of him. Now for it, he thought, and he began to undress her with his eyes. He expected her to blush and walk away as the young girls had done but she didn't do it. Instead her lips parted and her eyes grew wide, and he started to feel he might have bitten off more than he could chew, but he made sure he didn't let it show and - always useful in an emergency - gave her a mocking smile.

Instead of embarrassing her it seemed to

encourage her, though, and he began to quiver inside. The other females he had encountered had left the field by now, but the mature widow wasn't going anywhere and sooner or later he would have to say something. Mocking smiles and sardonic laughs were all right for the most part but they couldn't last forever.

Just as he was about to make a complete fool of himself by saying something like, 'Do you come here often?' she saved him from himself by glancing at the fob watch which hung across the front of his waistcoat.

Looking up at him archly she said, 'Have you got the time?'

He was so relieved at the ordinariness of her question that he didn't catch the way her tone of voice was suggestive and he completely missed the double nature of her words. Instead he latched on to the subject of his watch. She had obviously been admiring it, he thought in his confused state, and it would give him something to talk about.

'Yes, I have,' he said, and he saw her eyes grow wide again.

Good, he'd got her interested. The watch had been a good move, then. He pulled it out and looked at it. 'I always have the time,' he said.

Her eyes widened still further and he felt ready to explode with joy. Everything was going even better than he had expected. He'd thought it would be difficult to talk to women in his role of a rake, but it wasn't so hard after all.

'It's an expert time keeper,' he said, looking down at his watch. 'I got it in Paris. It strikes the hour and the minute, you know, if I want it to.'

He stopped talking. She was starting to smile at him but not in a way he liked. She was starting to smile at him in the way that women smiled at small children when the children had done something adorable. It was the way women had always smiled at him in the past, before he'd become a rake.

'There are only fifteen or twenty men in the whole of Paris who could make a watch like this,' he babbled, thinking he must get her interest back again and get it back quickly, before he went to pieces altogether.

'How sweet,' she said, and she laughed.

Oh, no! he thought. He could feel himself breaking out into a sweat. Not sweet! Rakes aren't meant to be sweet! If I'm not careful, she'll start patting me on the head in a minute!

She didn't do that, but what she did was almost worse. She patted him on the cheek instead.

'You look the part, but you've a lot to learn,' she said. 'Come and see me in five years time, when you've grown into your role. I promise you it will be worth it.' And with that she gave a mocking smile of her own and walked off.

Lizzie, standing behind the pillar from where she had been listening to every word, groaned. Oh, no, not even Alex would tell a sultry widow all about his watch! she thought. But she was wrong because she had just heard him doing it!

There was only one thing for it. She'd have to get him back to the inn before he did himself any more damage.

'Pssst,' she said.

Alex took no notice. He was too busy watching the widow's swaying hips as she walked across the ballroom and wondering what had gone wrong.

'It's me,' said Lizzie in a loud whisper. 'Don't look round but I'm behind the pillar.'

'Oh, thank the Lord,' said Alex, starting to walk round the pillar to join her.

'No! stay where you are,' she hissed. 'I said "don't look round", not "come and join me!" If anyone sees you walking round the pillar to talk to me it will make you look ridiculous. You're meant to be a careless rake, not someone who turns to his friends when things go wrong.'

'But I've already blown it,' he said. But he stayed where he was and whispered round the pillar, at the same time trying not to move his lips in case anyone was watching him. 'I just — '

'I know what you did, I was here the whole time. I heard every word, but don't worry, its not a complete disaster, you can still save the situation. Just cast a few more mocking glances round the room as though nothing dreadful's happened, and then if the widow tells anyone about the disastrous conversation she's just had with you, everyone will assume she's making it up out of spite because you weren't impressed with her charms. Now, do exactly what I tell you to. First, laugh sardonically in her direction, as though she's the one who's just made a fool of herself and not you.'

She waited until he'd done it.

'Now, swagger out of the room and go back to The King's Head. I'll bring the girls there tomorrow morning and we'll decide what's the best thing to do.'

She waited behind the pillar whilst Alex laughed sardonically and swaggered out of the room, and then she went to join Jane and Sophy, who were sipping glasses of champagne at the other end of the Assembly Rooms.

'What happened?' asked Sophy eagerly.

'It looked very interesting, but we couldn't tell what was going on from here,' said Jane.

Lizzie didn't know whether to laugh or cry. 'The widow wanted more than mocking smiles, and he didn't know what to do. And really, it was very difficult. There was no way he could stay in character unless he took her up on her offer and of course he didn't want to do that — '

'I wonder why not, she's very attractive,' said Sophy musingly, 'and Alex is a man after all.'

'He'd never be interested in someone like that,' said Lizzie, thinking a moment later, Goodness! why did I snap at Sophy like that?

Sophy looked at her strangely.

'He's only pretending, remember,' said Lizzie, getting a hold of herself. 'He's not really a rake. Besides, Lavinia's far too old for him if you want to know the truth.'

'She looks like a man-eater,' said Jane, her eyes following the sultry widow. 'I'm surprised she let him get away. How did he manage to get out of it in one piece?'

'It was easy, actually. He told her about his watch!'

'His watch?' asked Sophy in astonishment.

'Oh, no!' groaned Jane. 'Not his Breuget watch? The one he was so proud of when he brought it back from Paris?'

'Yes, that one,' said Lizzie. 'And that's not all, he told her all about where he got it, what it can do and what it can't do.'

Sophy shook her head in despair. 'It wasn't too hard to make him look like a rake, but we're never going to get him to behave like one, it's just not Alex.'

'Oh, well, he didn't look bothered by it,' said Jane. 'At least he didn't go to pieces.'

'That's because I was behind the pillar telling him what to do,' said Lizzie.

'Don't tell me you were listening to everything?' asked Sophy accusingly.

'Of course I was. I thought he could do with some help.'

'And what did you tell him to do?' asked Jane curiously.

'I told him to laugh it off, as though she was the one who'd made a fool of herself.'

'Yes, that was what it looked like,' Sophy agreed.

'Oh, good, then it worked. Now if we're careful it can all be smoothed over and then there'll be no harm done.'

Chapter Eleven

Now why did they do that? thought James as the girls hurried out of the dining-room on the following morning, straight after breakfast.

He thought of the strange atmosphere there'd been at the breakfast table. It had all been normal at the beginning, with the girls and his mother tucking into hot rolls and chocolate, and his father and him eating a hearty breakfast of ham and beef, but then his mother had asked them what they were doing that morning and the girls had looked decidedly shady. Sophy had squirmed in her seat and then she'd said they were going into town to do some shopping, but when he'd offered to go with them they'd made lots of excuses.

'We don't want to stop you going riding,' Jane had said. 'We know how much you like your exercise in the morning.'

'We don't want to bore you,' Lizzie had said at the same time.

'That's right. We'll be spending the morning looking at bonnets and ribbons and things,' Sophy had chimed in. 'You know how you hate it when you have to wait for me to try a bonnet on, and this time it'll be even worse because there'll be three of us.'

That had made him suspicious straight away, because Sophy was never worried about him being bored, she had dragged him off to town with her to help her buy a bonnet more times than he cared to remember, and she had never once worried that he might not be interested. Yes, there was something definitely suspicious about it.

For a minute he wondered if it could have anything to do with the rake who'd walked into the Assembly Rooms the evening before, and he wondered if they could have arranged a meeting with him. But then he shook his head. That wouldn't be like Sophy, and it wouldn't be like Jane either, he hoped - although why he should hope it he couldn't imagine.

He started thinking about the unknown rake. There'd been something odd about him. What was he doing in a small town in an out of the way corner of Kent? Men like that spent their time in London, at all the most fashionable balls, not in boring parts of the country. It was very odd, but he had a strange feeling that the girls knew him. There had been something about their expressions when the rake had swaggered into the ballroom that looked as though they'd seen him before. He wondered if they'd met the rake in London, but if that was it, then why didn't they say so?

And that was another thing. What were the girls really doing in Kent? He didn't believe they'd come to the country because there was an outbreak of measles. No, there'd been something shifty about Sophy when she'd said it, and he was certain it was just an excuse.

Oh, well, whatever it was, he'd find out eventually. He'd just have to be patient, that was all.

'I thought we'd never get away,' said Sophy with a deep sigh as the three girls walked into town.

'Me neither,' said Lizzie. She bit her lip. 'I'm not very happy about James. You don't think he's suspicious, do you? He was giving us very odd looks at breakfast, and I thought he was going to insist on coming shopping with us. I was very relieved when he didn't. But I think he might suspect something.'

'I wouldn't be surprised,' Sophy said. 'I'm sure he didn't believe my story about an outbreak of measles in London, and now with this on top of it he's definitely going to think something's going on.'

'If he's suspicious, wouldn't it be better to take him into our confidence and tell him all about it?' Jane asked.

'No,' said Lizzie, shaking her head. 'We can't take the risk.'

'But I'm sure it would be all right, James seems very trustworthy,' argued Jane.

'How can you know that?' asked Lizzie in surprise. 'You've only just met him.'

'Jane's right, all the same,' said Sophy. 'James likes mischief, but he's as trustworthy as they come. I agree with Lizzie, though, the fewer people who know about Alex the better.' She stopped walking as they went into the town. 'Now, you know what you've got to do?'

The girls nodded. They each had to play their part. Jane was going to visit the milliner's, as the lady who ran the establishment was a notorious gossip and would have all the news on the Assembly Rooms ball. Lizzie was going to visit the draper's, another den of gossip, and Sophy was to visit her cousin who lived in the manor house, and who would be sure to know what everyone was saying about Alex's run-in with the glorious widow.

'And when we've found out everything we can about what people are saying, we'll go to The King's Head and give Alex the news,' Lizzie said.

Alex paced the sitting-room of his private suite of apartments, waiting for the girls to arrive. If only he hadn't blown it last night. He groaned as he thought what a fool he'd made of himself, but as Lizzie had said, the situation might not be as bad as he thought, and besides, in the end it didn't really matter. It wasn't what happened in Kent that was important, it was what went on in London. He was only here to practise so that he didn't make a fool of himself when he went to London, after all.

Even so, he was relieved when Lizzie's first words to him as she walked into the room were, 'Cheer up. It's good news.'

'Hooray,' he said.

'We've been all round the town this morning talking to all the greatest gossips, and even though Lavinia Granville-Staples told everyone what went on, no one believed a word of it.'

'They all think it's sour grapes because Lavinia wanted you and couldn't have you,' said Sophy.

'You see, I told you it would be all right as long as you didn't lose your nerve and saw it through,' said Lizzie.

'Even so, it was awful.' Alex groaned, remembering the terrible conversation. 'One minute she was looking at me like I was a succulent steak, the next minute she was smiling kindly at me as though I was an adorable infant and patting me on the cheek.'

'She didn't!' exclaimed Lizzie. 'I didn't see her do that. How funny!'

'Not for me, it wasn't,' said Alex.

'You've only yourself to blame,' laughed Sophy, settling herself down on the sofa, with one leg tucked underneath her as usual. 'Imagine telling her about your watch. Whatever made you do such a thing?'

'It's interesting,' protested Alex. 'You were all interested when I told you about it, just after coming back from Paris last year. You wanted to know everything: how it was made, where I got it from and how it worked.'

Lizzie rolled her eyes. 'Yes, but we're your friends. We find everything you say interesting - well, nearly everything,' she said, not wanting him to get big-headed. 'But Lavinia isn't your friend. She's something else entirely.'

'Exactly,' said Jane. 'Just think how interesting you'd find it if Arabella told you all about her watch,' she said, with a dimple twitching at the corner of her mouth.

'Arabella hasn't got a watch,' said Alex.

'Well, if she had.'

'I'd think anything Arabella said was interesting,' he said confidently.

'Would you?' asked Lizzie. She had the strangest sinking feeling. Now why should that be? She shouldn't be getting a sinking feeling. She wasn't on a ship!

'No, you wouldn't, you wouldn't be listening to her at all. You'd be too busy looking at her beautiful face and thinking about her ample charms instead,'

Sophy told him.

'Well, maybe I would, but I certainly wouldn't smile at her in that superior way and pat her on the cheek, whatever I thought about her conversation,' grumbled Alex.

'But then you're not thirty yet,' said Jane, 'and Mrs Granville-Staples is.'

'All right, I can see it might have been a mistake to talk about my watch, but I don't see what I should have said instead.'

'That's easy,' said Sophy. 'You should have picked up on her suggestiveness — '

'How do you know about that?'

'Lizzie was listening from behind the pillar — '

'And shouldn't have been,' interrupted Alex.

'It's a good thing I was, or you'd be a laughing stock by now,' said Lizzie. 'If I hadn't heard what you said, I wouldn't have been able to help you save the situation.'

'Then you should have said something cutting,' went on Sophy as though she'd never been interrupted. 'Something that would have put Mrs Granville-Staples in her place.'

'I know that,' said Alex, 'but I couldn't think of anything on the spur of the moment. What do I do if someone asks me if I've got the time again?'

The girls thought about it.

Then Jane's face cleared. 'I've got it. When Lavinia said, "Do you have the time?" you should have said, "Yes, I do . . . " Then you should have given her a mocking smile and added ". . . but not for you."'

'Before walking off with a mocking smile on

your face,' said Sophy.

'Yes,' said Lizzie. 'That would have been very good. So remember it in case you need it again.'

'And what if someone doesn't ask me if I've got the time?'

'What do you mean?' Sophy asked.

'What if they don't say anything? I was lucky in a way that Mrs Granville-Staples did speak to me, because I would have blurted out something even more idiotic if she hadn't. The silence was getting embarrassing.'

'Did you try undressing her with your eyes?' asked Lizzie.

'I tried everything, but nothing made her blush and nothing made her run away, which left me wondering what to do next.'

'He has a point,' said Jane. 'He can't go on smiling and laughing for ever.'

'It's difficult,' said Lizzie. 'But I don't think you're ready for conversation yet.'

'Then what do I do if I'm put on the spot?'

'If you're put on the spot - well, then, just take the lady's hand, kiss it slowly, give her a mocking smile and walk away.'

'That's good,' said Jane. 'It will cover any situation.'

'I'm going to have to learn how to make conversation at some point. It's all right with people here, but I can't keep walking away from Arabella once we get to London or it will defeat the whole purpose of my becoming a rake.'

'You'll have learnt a lot by then,' Lizzie reassured him — oh no! she was reassuring him again! 'And besides, behaving like a rake is only to get her interested in you in the first place. Once you've caught her attention you can say what you like. Just make sure you've caught her first.'

'Ask her to marry you as soon as you can,' put in Sophy, 'then it won't put too great a strain on you, because once it's too late for her to back out you can stop being a rake and start being yourself.'

Alex frowned. There seemed to be something wrong with Sophy's logic. It made it seem like he was going to trap Arabella into marrying him when what he really wanted to do was to sweep her off her feet. But then what?

An image of her wonderful white bosom rose before him and he knew what he wanted to do once he'd swept her off her feet. But a nagging voice inside him asked, And once you've enjoyed her charms, what then? Luckily, he managed to silence it. There was no use trying to run before he could walk, as Lizzie had told him. First he had to pique Arabella's interest. He could worry about what to say to her afterwards.

'There's no need to go to those lengths,' said Lizzie hurriedly. 'Marriage is a big step, you don't want to rush into it. Besides, we've come up with some ways to make you even more attractive. It would be a shame to propose to her before you've had a chance to try them out.'

'You have?' asked Alex. His attention was caught.

'Yes. We'll tell you all about it tomorrow. It's the last stage in turning you into someone Arabella can't resist. But we can't stay now. We have to be going or else Sophy's aunt will be wondering where we are.' She almost added, 'And James is already suspicious', but decided against it. The last thing Alex needed was to be worrying that his cover might be about to be blown.

'We'll meet you on the downs in the morning, at nine o'clock,' went on Lizzie, 'and then we'll tell you the plan.'

'All right,' said Alex. 'I'll leave everything to you.'

Chapter Twelve

Alex frowned as he got ready to go out riding once the girls had left. There was something that had been bothering him ever since talking to the girls and he couldn't think what it was. It was something to do with not talking to Arabella properly until after they were engaged.

His thoughts had never been very definite before. He had just known he wanted to take Arabella in his arms and press her sweet lips to his, but once he started to talk to her, as he would have to do at some time, what would it be about? Even once he wasn't pretending to be a rake and could just be himself he wouldn't know what to say to her. He'd tried to talk to her before quite a few times, but words had always failed him. He'd thought it was because he had been overcome by her beauty, but now he wasn't so sure.

There was something else that was bothering him as well, and that was the memory of Lord and Lady Halston. Lord and Lady Halston were neighbours of his, and they lived on a nearby estate in Cambridgeshire. They were an odd couple. They never looked at each other or talked to each other, in fact they were like two separate people and not man and wife at all. He had asked his father why on earth they had got married in the first place if they had nothing to say to each other and his father had said, 'Well, Lady Halston was very beautiful.'

He thought it over as he slipped into his coat, and he realized that that was one of the things bothering him. Arabella was like Lady Halston, she was very beautiful, with her blue eyes and her guinea-gold curls, but that didn't mean she'd make him a perfect wife. Beauty didn't last for ever, and even if it did, it seemed a poor sort of thing to have to live the way Lord and Lady Halston lived, never speaking to each other and never doing things together, just living under the same roof in what passed for some kind of harmony.

I could always take a mistress, he thought, if Arabella and I didn't get along.

But then, what was the point of that? He was never likely to find a mistress more beautiful than Arabella, and if he took someone he could get along with as his mistress, then that would make her more like his wife than Arabella, which made a nonsense of the whole thing.

Besides, he didn't like the idea of taking a mistress. He didn't like that sort of life at all, he came from a close family and when he got married he wanted his own family to be the same, with him and his wife tending the estate and raising a parcel of happy, rumbustious children who'd carry on the family tradition and look after it in their turn.

He couldn't see Arabella as the mother of rumbustious children no matter how hard he tried. In fact, strange to say, he couldn't see Arabella as the mother of his children at all. But that, of course, must be because she hadn't agreed to marry him yet.

There was no use worrying about it at the moment. Arabella probably wouldn't give him a second glance anyway, even if he was dressed as a rake, so why plague himself with worries about the sort of wife she'd make? There was time enough for that later.

And if she did look at him, well, then, why did he have to imagine the worst? What was the point of him worrying about them not getting along when he hardly knew the girl? It was bound to be awkward at first, but once the ice was broken things would be different, he was sure of it. For all he knew, they might get on like a house on fire. After all, he and Lizzie got on really well so why shouldn't he get on as well with Arabella?

Yes. Why not?

He finished dressing, then he glanced out of the window and saw that it was raining. Oh, well, he'd just have to go riding tomorrow instead.

'I'm not sure,' said Sophy with a frown as the girls went downstairs after they left Alex. 'It seems like an awful risk to me.'

'But we have to tell someone,' argued Lizzie, 'because we need another man for our plan.'

'But I don't think it should be James,' said Sophy.

'Why not?' asked Jane. 'You said yourself that he was trustworthy. In that case, he's the perfect choice.'

'I'm still not sure,' said Sophy.

'Is it because you think he won't agree to help us?' asked Lizzie.

'No.' Sophy shook her head. 'James likes mischief as much as anyone, I'm sure he'll be willing to help, but it's just that I think the fewer people who know the truth about Alex the better.'

'Someone has to know,' Lizzie pointed out.

'Otherwise we can't go through with it.'

'But if it was an outsider, then we wouldn't have to tell him the whole thing. As long as we paid him well, we could tell him a bit and not tell him about Alex's transformation. That way, news of it could never get back to Arabella.'

'Then you don't trust James,' said Jane accusingly.

'Of course I do. But he might let something slip.'

'Is he going to London, then?' asked Lizzie, chewing her bottom lip.

'Yes, he goes every year. My aunt and uncle will be going, too, but only for a short while. They like to go up for a few weeks, but after that my aunt misses the country and they come home again. But James likes it there, and so he stays.'

'If we tell him how important it is, I'm sure he'll watch his tongue,' said Jane.

'And he's still our best hope,' said Lizzie. 'If we pay someone to do it, they might run away with the money and leave us stranded.'

'Or go too far, and hurt someone,' Jane pointed out. 'The type of person we could hire to play that kind of part wouldn't be too nice in their scruples, and they might easily ruin the whole thing.'

They had by this time reached the bottom of the stairs.

'Wait here,' said Sophy. 'I'll check the coast is clear.'

She slipped across the hall and glanced into the public rooms opening off it to make sure they could pass without being seen. Three girls shouldn't really be at the inn by themselves, and people would talk if anyone noticed them. Luckily it was a quiet time of day and no one was about. She waved to the others, so they crossed the hall and went out of the door.

'Made it,' said Lizzie. 'I always feel better when we've managed to get in and out.'

'Well, well,' came a voice behind them.

They froze.

'Oh, no. Rumbled,' said Sophy.

They turned round, and they saw James standing there with a determined look on his face.

'Now then, I suggest you tell me all about it,' he said.

'About what?' Sophy blustered.

'About visiting The King's Head without mother and father knowing, and without even taking your maid.'

'It looks like we'll have to tell him now,' said Lizzie to the other girls.

'Yes,' said Jane. 'It's time we told James.'

'Well?' he asked, raising his eyebrows and looking at Sophy. 'I'd like to know what you've been doing, coz. Why did you make up that ridiculous story about the measles, and why did you come down to Kent? I want to know where you've been getting to on your 'visits to town' - although I suppose that question's been answered,' he said, looking up at the sign of The King's Head. 'And most of all, what are you doing spending your time with a scandalous rake?'

'Well!' he said, fifteen minutes later, when they had explained. 'So he's one of your friends?' He let out a low whistle. 'Even so, he isn't quite the thing.'

'But that's just what we've been trying to explain

to you,' said Sophy. 'He isn't usually like that, but he wanted us to turn him into a rake in order to impress Arabella, so we gave him some help and now that's what he is.'

'He looks like a rake, anyway,' put in Lizzie. 'But he's not a rake in the way he behaves, that's just an act to help him impress young ladies.'

'You mean he doesn't usually swagger into ballrooms and glower at everyone?' asked James.

'No,' said Lizzie. 'He's usually like you.'

'Really?' James's eyes lit up. 'So that means I could look like that too if I wanted to?' His eyes took on a dreamy expression.

'I suppose so,' said Sophy, 'but that's not the point. The point is we need your help, so will you do it? Will you help us?'

'I might do,' he said teasingly. 'But what's in it for me?'

'Well, of all the . . . ' Sophy spluttered. 'I never thought I'd see the day when — '

'Adventure,' said Lizzie, interrupting her.

'Excitement,' said Jane. She looked at him critically. 'I think you'd look very good in the part.'

'Really?' asked James with interest.

Jane nodded. 'Really.'

'Well, I don't know,' he said, appearing to think it over. Then he grinned and said: 'All right, I'll do it.'

Chapter Thirteen

'I told you it would be a good idea to get James on our side,' said Jane as they walked to the downs for their meeting with Alex. 'I knew he'd understand.'

'I don't call going as red as a turkey-cock before laughing hysterically understanding,' said Sophy.

'I don't know why you're so down on James,' said Jane. 'He was perfectly wonderful about the whole thing. You can't blame him for being amused to begin with, but as soon as he knew how serious it was he couldn't wait to help.'

'That's true,' said Lizzie. 'It was nice of him to offer to help us, it will make things so much easier. I never liked the idea of hiring someone, there were so many problems with the idea, but now we have James on our side, I think our plan should work.'

'Oh, look, there's Alex now,' said Jane.

The three of them waved to Alex, who was waiting for them where they'd arranged to meet, and soon afterwards they joined him.

'Well?' he said, once their greetings were over with. 'Don't keep me in the dark, tell me, Lizzie, what's your plan?'

'It's very simple, really,' said Lizzie, holding on to her bonnet with one hand, because although the sun was shining, there was a strong breeze blowing, and she didn't want it to blow away. 'You're finding it difficult to talk to women at the moment, so what you need is a way of impressing women without ever having to open your mouth, and that's what I've come up with. It's all very well to look the part, but this is something even better.'

She paused.

'Well?' said Alex impatiently.

'My idea is for you to practise rescuing someone from a dangerous situation. The beauty of the scheme is that if you're rescuing her from something difficult, you won't have to think of anything to talk to her about, she'll be so grateful to you for your help that she won't expect conversation.'

'There's only one thing wrong with that idea,' said Alex, whose greatcoat was flapping in the breeze. 'There aren't any dangerous situations in Kent, or in London either for that matter. The war against Napoleon is over, and there aren't likely to be any dangerous situations in the future either. If Napoleon had gone ahead and invaded us like he always threatened to do I might have been able to save a young lady from a marauding French soldier or a leering French officer, but in peace time it just won't work. Sorry, Lizzie, it's a nice idea, but there it is.'

'You don't need a war in order to rescue someone,' said Sophy. 'You could always rescue someone who's sprained her ankle. If a young lady fell over and twisted it you could ride up on a white charger — '

'I haven't got a white charger,' he interrupted. 'All my horses are black.'

'That's a really small problem, not worth worrying about. So as I was saying, you could ride up on a white charger,' she went on, 'sweep her up into your arms, put her up in front of you on the saddle and take her home.'

'And then, once you'd taken her home, you could carry her into the house and put her on the sofa. Then you could smile scornfully when she and her mother tried to thank you, and ride off again,' said Jane.

'But I've never met a young lady who's sprained her ankle in my life, so I'm not likely to fall over one in the next ten days,' said Alex. 'And even if I did it wouldn't help me with Arabella. I can't see her spraining her ankle when I just happen to be riding by, and if by some miracle she did, she'd be sure to have a companion and a footman to take her back to the house and so she wouldn't need me at all.'

'That's not the point,' said Sophy. 'If you get used to helping damsels in distress, then if a chance to help Arabella crops up, you'll know what to do. Admit it, if we hadn't told you what to do and Arabella had sprained her ankle you wouldn't have thought of sweeping her off her feet and carrying her back home again, now would you?'

'The footman — '

'Never mind the footman. Rakes don't go around bothering about footmen. They act as if there are no such things as footmen. And never mind the companion either. If you're lucky enough for it to happen, don't listen to any protests, just sweep Arabella off her feet, refuse to listen to any objections, and carry her masterfully home.'

'All right, if you say so, but I can't see it happening in the next few weeks, so how am I to get any practise?'

'We've already thought of that,' said Lizzie, 'and there is a way. Do you know Miss Melody Vauxhall?'

'No. Was she at the Assembly Rooms ball?'

'Yes, she was. She was the young lady in the white satin gown with a green silk bodice.'

'The one with the auburn hair?' queried Alex.

'Yes, that's the one. She looked up when you entered the room and after that she couldn't take her eyes off you — '

'Really?' Alex smirked.

'Really,' said Lizzie firmly. 'But there's no need to smirk. That was the idea after all, to have young ladies looking at you. Well, we've decided you're going to rescue Miss Vauxhall from a vicious footpad.'

Alex looked at her as if she were queer in the attic. Then he looked round at the other girls, and as soon as he saw their enthusiastic faces he gave a groan. 'I knew it had to happen sooner or later, you've all run stark staring mad. You're each of you as bad as the other. I'll be coming to visit you in an asylum before you know it.'

'Don't talk nonsense,' said Lizzie in exasperation. 'Of course we're not mad.'

'Oh no? Then answer me the following questions. One: why on earth would Melody Vauxhall be attacked by a footpad? This is a really quiet neighbourhood, and I shouldn't be surprised if it hasn't seen a footpad for twenty years. Two: even if she was attacked by a footpad, how on earth would I just happen to be in the right place at the right time? Three: even if I was in the right place at the right time, how would I manage to rescue her - that is the plan, I suppose, that I should rescue her?'

The girls nodded.

'Then how would I manage to rescue her,' he went on, 'without getting myself killed in the process?'

'Is that all?' asked Lizzie.

'Isn't that enough?' he said.

'No, it isn't. One: Melody will be attacked because we'll arrange for it to happen. Two: you will be in the right place at the right time because we'll know when and where the attack is going to take place, and you will be waiting for it. Three: you will be able to rescue her because her attacker will be James in disguise.'

'James?' Alex looked horrified. 'Oh, no, you're not letting James in on this,' he said, shaking his head.

Lizzie shifted uncomfortably.

'You haven't already done it?'

'It wasn't Lizzie's fault,' said Sophy. 'He guessed something was up and so he waylaid us outside The King's Head yesterday afternoon. We had to tell him, otherwise he would have told my aunt and uncle we were mixing with bad company and it would all have come out then, anyway.'

Alex groaned.

'I knew coming to Kent was a bad idea,' he said.

'Nonsense,' returned Lizzie. 'You didn't know any such thing.'

'Anyway, it's a good thing James does know,' said Jane, 'because once he understood how serious it was he offered to help us, which means that he will be our footpad and attack Melody on her way home from her grandmother's.'

'Then you'll leap in and rescue her,' said Lizzie.

'James will put up a convincing struggle before letting you punch him on the nose and then you can run off with Miss Vauxhall into the sunset.'

'Or the sunrise.'

'Or the pouring rain, more likely,' said Sophy with a laugh.

Lizzie glared at Sophy, then she turned back to Alex. 'Miss Vauxhall will be grateful and fall in love with you on the spot,' she said.

'No,' he said firmly. 'Absolutely not. I don't like the idea one little bit. I'm not going to have Miss Vauxhall frightened just so that I can come along and rescue her, it simply isn't fair, I'm surprised you could even think about it.'

'Melody Vauxhall isn't frightened of anything,' said Sophy with a snort. 'When the Vauxhalls had burglars at their house last year, Melody chased them down the garden in her nightdress. She was waving her father's shotgun and she scared them off so completely that they were never seen in the neighbourhood again.'

'Then she won't need me to rescue her,' said Alex. 'It sounds to me like she can look after herself.'

Lizzie nodded. 'Yes, she can, most of the time, but she'll need you to rescue her this time, because this time she won't have a shotgun with her.'

'Besides,' said Sophy, 'she'll want to be grateful.'

Alex looked surprised. 'Why?'

'Because you'll be every girl's dream come true. You'll be young, handsome and rakish and on top of all that you'll be rescuing her from danger. She's not going to ruin a perfectly good rescue by fixing matters herself.'

'It isn't so much that she'll be grateful to you for rescuing her, so much as that she'll be grateful to you for acting like a hero out of a story book,' explained Jane. 'It's very romantic, and it will give her something to dream about until she's old and grey.'

This made Alex keep quiet about his next objection, which was that even if Miss Vauxhall wasn't frightened it wouldn't be fair to use her as a dupe, but if it was going to give her something to dream about until she was old and grey then it was nothing to be ashamed of. In fact, it might even be a good thing. It would give her something to tell her grandchildren. "My dear children," he could imagine her saying in a quavering voice, "when I was a young girl I was once attacked by a footpad, and then I was rescued by a handsome rake. I have remembered it all these years. I hope something as romantic as that happens to you when you grow up."

'Well, that's the plan,' said Lizzie. 'What do you think?'

Alex still didn't look convinced.

'It will give you some practise at being a maiden's prayer. and it will come in useful if anything unfortunate happens to Arabella,' Sophy coaxed him. 'You never know, there are footpads and highwaymen and pickpockets in London, and there might come a time when she needs defending from one of them. It would impress her if you knew how to take charge.'

'Oh, very well,' said Alex. He spoke reluctantly but he was secretly pleased with the plan. Although he would never have admitted it, he rather liked the idea of rescuing young ladies who would go on to dream about him for the rest of their lives.

'Then it's decided,' said Sophy. 'We'll tell James that we've decided to go ahead with it, and we'll let you know when everything's fixed.'

Chapter Fourteen

'It's going to take a lot of thinking about,' said Lizzie. She pulled her knees up to her chest as she sat on the window seat in the library, working out the details of the plan with Sophy, Jane and James. 'We'll only get one shot at it. We've got to make sure it works first time.'

'We need to go over the ground, and we need to work out exactly where the attack is going to take place,' said Sophy. 'It's a pity it's raining, otherwise we could do it today.'

'It will just have to wait,' said Lizzie. 'Meanwhile, there are other things we can see to — '

'Such as, what am I going to wear?' said James.

'Something rough,' said Sophy.

James looked rebellious.

'Yes,' said Jane, looking at him thoughtfully. 'Some rough workmen's clothes would suit you. If you had a black handkerchief tied round the lower half of your face, you'd really look quite dashing, it would show up your dark hair and the colour of your eyes.'

'Really?' he asked. He gave Jane a lingering look.

'Really,' said Sophy firmly. 'The question is, where are you going to find some rough clothes and a black handkerchief?'

'There must be something that would do in the dressing-up box,' said Jane. 'You do have a dressing-up box?' she asked, turning to James.

'Yes, there's one in the attic. We used to use it as children.'

'The clothes won't be big enough,' said Lizzie with a frown.

'Yes, they will,' said James. 'They were mostly old clothes belonging to my grandmother and grandfather. The boys used to roll the sleeves up and the girls used to pin the skirts up to make them fit.'

'Good. Then that's where we'll begin.'

They went up to the attics and rummaged through the dressing-up clothes.

'Goodness, did our grandmothers really wear clothes like this?' asked Sophy as she held up a stomacher, and 'No wonder they used to have to turn sideways to get through doorways,' said Jane, as she tried on a wide pair of panniers.

They finally found what they were looking for.

'Try them on,' said Jane, as James held up a tattered pair of breeches and a shabby black coat.

James went behind a Chinese screen, which had been put in the attic as it was broken, and tried on the clothes. He came out from behind the screen a few minutes later looking just like a rogue.

'Now try on the handkerchief,' said Jane.

He folded it in half, then tied the triangular piece of material over the lower half of his face.

'Perfect,' said Sophy.

He turned to Jane. 'What do you think?' he asked.

'Yes,' she agreed. 'Perfect.'

'Good,' said Lizzie decidedly. 'That's one problem solved. Now you just need a hat — '

'There's a tricorne in here somewhere,' said

Sophy, rummaging through the box once again. 'I saw it here - ah, yes, here it is.'

She held up the three-cornered hat.

'It's a bit old-fashioned,' said Lizzie dubiously. 'No one wears tricornes any more.'

'It doesn't have to be in the height of fashion,' said Sophy practically. 'He isn't going to walk down Bond Street.'

'Besides, a tricorne's easier to pull down,' said Jane. 'It will hide his face better, and complete the disguise.'

She took it from Sophy and handed it to James.

He put it on and pulled it firmly down at all three corners.

'Yes,' nodded Sophy. 'That will do very well.'

Once they had chosen his clothes, James went behind the screen again and changed back into his everyday coat and breeches.

'Do you know,' said Lizzie, looking out of the window. 'I think the rain's stopped.

'Then we'd better check out the lay of the land, and decide where Melody's going to be waylaid,' said Sophy.

'I've got to go to the stables to check up on one of the mares, she's taken a nasty fall and I want to find out if she's going to be all right,' said James.

'You can join us when you've finished. In fact if you ride into the village and we walk, you'll be there almost as soon as us anyway,' said Sophy.

The girls dressed warmly in their outdoor things and then they set off.

'That was a really good idea of yours to tell James he'd look nice dressed up as a footpad, even if it was stretching the truth,' said Sophy to Jane. 'It made all the difference. I was worried that he was going to back out at one point.'

'It wasn't stretching the truth,' said Jane. 'I think he does look nice dressed up as a footpad. He has the loveliest eyes I've ever seen.'

'Don't tell me you're falling for James!' said Sophy with a laugh.

'No, of course not,' said Jane irritably. 'All I said was he had nice eyes.'

'Never mind his eyes. We're going to need our wits about us if we're going to choose the best spot for the attack,' Lizzie said.

It was cold and they walked briskly to keep out the March chill. The sun was shining but the air was very cold. There'd been frost that morning and some of it was still there, shining on the leaves and grass. It wasn't a long walk to the village and they were soon there.

'Melody comes to see her godmother every Tuesday and Thursday afternoon,' said Sophy. 'She's never on horseback, she always walks, and she's always on her own, which is perfect for our plan. She leaves her godmother's house - that's it over there, the one with the green door - and walks past the church and then over the common at three o'clock, as regular as clockwork.'

'That's useful to know,' said a voice behind them.

'James! You've got here.'

'How was the mare?' asked Jane.

'She's much better, thank you, the horse doctor's been to see her and he says she's going to be all right.'

'What was that you were saying about the possibilities?' asked Lizzie.

'I think it will be best if I attack her on the common,' said James.

'Yes,' said Sophy, 'that's the best plan. There are lots of trees and you can easily stay hidden amongst them until the last minute, before jumping out at her.'

'And Alex can stay hidden too, until it's time for him to come to the rescue,' Lizzie said.

'We'd better choose the exact spot,' said Jane.

They walked out of the village and then they took the left branch of the road which led them to the common. The common was a wide open space with scrubby grass and some wild daffodils blowing in the breeze. There were trees on either side, so it was perfect for their scheme.

'I think here would be a good spot,' said Lizzie, after she had given the matter a lot of thought and deliberation. 'Alex can hide behind that pile of logs over there until he's needed.'

'No,' said Sophy, 'he'll have to be riding a horse.'

Lizzie frowned. 'He won't be able to hide if he's riding a horse. I think we'd better settle for him saving her on foot.'

'It will be all right if he waits well back from the track and hides in the fir trees,' said Sophy.

The common had a clump of fir trees in the middle of it which still had their needles, not like the deciduous trees round about that had lost their leaves, and it would be easy for a man and horse to hide in there.

'Won't she hear it?' asked Lizzie, thinking that a horse might complicate things, no matter how good an idea it seemed.

'It won't matter if she does. People ride horses across the common all the time. She won't think anything's wrong if she hears one neighing in the distance.'

'Well, all right, then, he can hide in the clump of fir trees, so I think you had better jump out at Melody over here,' she said to James. She pointed out the spot.

James nodded. There was a bend in the track just ahead of the spot Lizzie had chosen which would keep him hidden until the last minute, then he'd come loping round it and grab hold of Melody's arm.

'Then, when she's struggled a bit, you'll need to grab hold of her reticule, that will make it seem like you're a proper footpad. It will be good for Alex, too, because as soon as he sees you grab the reticule he will know it's time for him to ride to the rescue.'

'Then what's going to happen?' asked James dubiously.

'Then he'll leap off his horse, punch you on the nose and rescue Melody,' said Sophy triumphantly.

'That's all very well for Alex, but it's not very good for me,' said James. 'I don't fancy having someone punch me on the nose.'

'It will only be play acting,' said Sophy. 'You can practise a bit first so it looks convincing, but you won't really get hurt.'

'I'd better not,' said James. 'I just hope Alex is going to be grateful for all this.'

'Oh, he is,' said Sophy.

'Well, it's all settled,' said Lizzie. 'We know what we're doing.'

'I can't walk out of the house in rough clothes,' said James. 'What if someone sees me?'

'You'll have to get changed in the gazebo,' said Sophy. 'You can leave your ordinary clothes there, and then you can change back again when you've done your bit, before you go into the house.'

'All right, I'll do that,' said James.

'Now all we have to do is explain it to Alex and then we're ready to go.'

Chapter Fifteen

'I'm still not keen on being punched on the nose,' complained James as he sat in Alex's private sitting-room with the three girls and Alex himself later that day. It was the one part of the adventure that he didn't like.

'Goodness, James, stop making such a fuss,' said Sophy in exasperation. 'Anyone would think Alex was going to try and hurt you. It's only play acting, you won't feel a thing.'

'You're going to have to practise it, though, if you're going to make it look convincing,' said Lizzie.

'And remember to pull your punch so you don't really hurt him,' said Jane to Alex.

'Now,' said Lizzie, standing up, 'I'll be Melody. I'll pretend to be walking along the common.' She took a few steps, but only a few, because the room wasn't very big. 'Now, you come round the corner, James.'

James jumped up out of his armchair and walked over to the far side of the room, then he turned round. He leaned forwards, scowling and looking menacing, and then he began to walk purposefully towards her.

'That's good,' said Lizzie encouragingly. 'Now, grab my arm and tug at my reticule, saying, "I'll take that, my beauty."'

'Oh, Lizzie! no one would say "I'll take that, my beauty!"' laughed Sophy. 'It may only be play acting to us, but Melody has to think it's real.'

'How do you know what a footpad would say?'

said Lizzie. 'Have you ever been attacked by one?'

Sophy had to admit that she had not.

'Well, then.' She turned back to James. 'Say, "I'll take that, my beauty", or something like it, anything you think sounds right. It doesn't really matter what words you use, as long as you grab Melody and then you demand her reticule.'

'I think I'll say, "I'll take that,"' said James, growling the words and getting into the spirit of the thing. 'And then I'll pull her reticule out of her hands, like this.'

He demonstrated with Lizzie's reticule.

'Careful!' said Lizzie, alarmed. 'That's my favourite reticule. I don't want it wrenched off its cord.'

'It has to look convincing,' said Jane to Lizzie reprovingly. 'I thought you did it very well,' she said to James.

'"Let's get back to business,' said Sophy. 'The reticule has been snatched - that's your cue, Alex. As soon as you see James take the reticule you come to the rescue.'

Alex looked awkward.

'I'll be on horseback, you say?'

'Yes.'

'You'll have to pretend for now,' said Lizzie.

He sighed. 'Oh, very well.' Looking a bit foolish he mimed galloping towards them, but by the time he'd mimed leaping off his horse he was thoroughly involved.

'That's good,' said Lizzie.

'But can you leap off a horse in real life?' asked Jane doubtfully. It was all very well trying things out in Alex's private sitting-room, but she wanted to make sure they'd work in real life.

'Of course he can,' said Lizzie. 'Alex is a really good rider.'

'All right, then,' said Jane.

'Then you say, "Unhand her",' said Sophy, bringing them back to the point.

'Do I have to?' groaned Alex.

'Yes.' All three girls chorused the answer.

He sighed. 'Oh, all right. Unhand her,' he said to James.

'You need to say it with more gusto,' said Lizzie.

'UNHAND HER!'

'Wonderful,' sighed Lizzie.

'Now. He refuses to let go of her,' said Sophy, 'and after a brief struggle you plant him a facer.'

'Be careful,' said Jane.

Alex made a pantomime of punching James, and James fell to the floor.

'That won't do.' Lizzie frowned. 'It doesn't look convincing. James, you can't just stand there when he hits you, you'll have to make a show of fighting back. Try it again.'

A brief scuffle followed.

'That's better,' Lizzie said.

'Now, when he hits you, stagger backwards to make it look more real before you fall over. It would be even better if you wiped your nose with your sleeve, as though you're wiping all the blood away, then picked yourself up, gave a frightened look at Alex and then ran away.'

'Melody won't see all that,' Alex said. 'She's meant to be looking at me, not James.'

'Even so, if she catches sight of James out of the corner of her eye he has to be convincing.'

They went through it again and James was by now as enthusiastic as the rest of them. He played his part to perfection.

'That's very good. Now, on to the next part of the drama.' Lizzie turned to Alex. 'This is where you have to sweep Melody off her feet.'

'I'm not sure about that.'

'Trust us,' said Sophy.

'Lift her into your arms, look smoulderingly into her eyes, then carry her masterfully off to your horse,' said Lizzie.

Alex was still not convinced. 'How heavy is she?' he asked.

'Good heavens! You can't be thinking about something like that at a moment like this,' declared Lizzie. 'It doesn't matter how heavy she is, you still have to carry her over to your horse. But don't worry, we've found you a placid animal. It won't wander off once you've leapt from its back, so you won't have to carry her too far.'

'And whatever you do, make sure you don't drop her,' giggled Sophy.

Alex cast her a withering look.

'Now,' said Lizzie, 'let's try it all the way through.'

James attacked her, Alex mimed leaping off his horse, spun James round, wrestled with him briefly, punched him on the nose, then swept Lizzie off her feet and carried her over to his horse. The horse, for the purposes of this afternoon, they had decided would be played by the chaise longue in the bedroom.

It was all going swimmingly, thought Lizzie, until Alex lifted her effortlessly into his arms. Then suddenly everything changed.

How peculiar, she thought as he strode towards the bedroom door. Everything seems to have gone very quiet. I can even hear myself breath.

The moment seemed to go on for ever. Time moved strangely slowly as though they were at the bottom of the sea, away from the real world in a time and space all their own. But when he set her on her feet again she felt the moment hadn't gone on long enough. She could have happily stayed in his arms for the rest of her life.

Her legs felt wobbly when he put her down. It was as if they'd turned to jelly. She half sat, half collapsed onto the edge of the chaise longue to stop herself from falling over.

I hope I'm not sickening for something, she thought. But although her legs felt like jelly it was really rather a nice sort of feeling, and besides, apart from her legs, she felt quite all right, so it was probably nothing, just one of those funny turns that happened sometimes.

'Well?' asked Alex, 'how did I do?'

There was something different about him, she thought as she looked at him. He looked older and more capable and more intense, he really had got it off very well. And all of a sudden she wished the burning look in his eyes had been for her instead of Arabella.

She brought herself back to reality and said, 'You did very well.' She reminded herself that Alex was her friend and nothing more, and besides, she wanted to help him catch Arabella. 'Melody Vauxhall will be like wax in your hands.'

'That was wonderful,' said Sophy, who had followed them into the bedroom with Jane and James behind her. She clasped her hands together and gave a long sigh. 'Why aren't there more rakes in the world? I'm envious of Melody already, and that's something I thought I'd never be. I want to be rescued by someone, too.'

Alex looked pleased at this, though for some reason he didn't look as pleased as he ought to be.

James scowled at all the attention Alex was getting, but he brightened up when Jane said, 'I thought you were really good. When you're dressed in your rough clothes with the handkerchief tied over your face you'll be very convincing.'

'Well, everything's ready,' said Lizzie, she was once more brisk and in control. 'We'll carry out our plan next Thursday. We will meet on the common at half-past two so that we have plenty of time to take our places before Melody appears at three o'clock.'

Chapter Sixteen

'At last!' said Lizzie with relief as she and Alex took their places on Thursday afternoon. 'We're ready. We've made all our preparations, and it's time to put our plan into action.'

Everything had been more difficult than she'd thought it was going to be. They hadn't been able to get hold of a white charger and so they had had to make do with a small white horse instead, but now they were all ready for the afternoon's adventure.

James was kitted out in the clothes borrowed from the dressing-up box, and he had the black silk handkerchief tied round his face. Jane and Sophy were watching from behind some bushes, and Lizzie was hiding with Alex in the stand of pine trees, together with the white horse, waiting for the excitement to begin.

'Three o'clock,' said Lizzie as the church clock chimed the hour, and the sound rang out over the common. 'Good. Melody should be along any minute.'

Sure enough, they didn't have long to wait before they saw Melody walking past. She was dressed in a red silk pelisse and she had a fetching bonnet perched on her head. She was carrying a red silk reticule and she was swinging it by its strings.

'Good,' said Lizzie in a low voice to Alex. 'I was half afraid she wouldn't have her reticule with her and then our plan wouldn't have worked, but I needn't have worried. She's not just carrying it, she's swinging it all over the place, so nothing should go wrong.'

Melody was still walking along, not knowing anything about the adventure that was going to happen to her. Then from round the corner came James, looking suitably villainous, and Lizzie held her breath as she watched him walk menacingly towards Melody.

'Make this easy on yourself,' he growled as he grabbed her arm and held it tight. 'Just give me your reticule and you won't get hurt.'

Alex was hiding in the pine trees, and as soon as he saw James grab Melody, he climbed on his white horse. He was just going to set off to the rescue when Lizzie held him back.

'Give James another minute or two,' she whispered. 'The longer Melody has to wait to be rescued, the more grateful she will be when it finally happens.'

They saw Melody struggle to wrench her arm free, and they saw James holding on tight.

Lizzie was just about to say, 'Now!' and send Alex on his way, when suddenly Melody stamped on James's foot and James let out a startled cry. He was so surprised that he let go of her arm.

'Oh, no, now she's going to run off,' groaned Lizzie.

But not a bit of it. Melody was swinging her reticule above her head. She swung it once, then twice, then three times to build up momentum, and then she finally let it go and struck James a resounding blow on the side of the head.

'Goodness,' said Lizzie. 'I never thought she'd

do that. It's lucky it's only a reticule she's hit him with, at least he can't be hurt.'

But contrary to her words James staggered backwards with the force of the blow and fell over, landing unceremoniously on his behind.

'Oh no!' groaned Alex, as the white horse champed at the bit.

Their carefully-laid plan was quickly falling to pieces. Instead of waiting for him to rescue her, Melody had rescued herself and she was now straightening her shoulders and tugging down smartly on the front of her pelisse, and looking for all the world like someone who knew how to handle trouble instead of like a damsel in distress who needed a knight on a white charger to ride to her rescue.

She uttered a loud 'Humph!' before saying in disgust, 'They don't make footpads like they used to,' then she went on her way.

'Oh, dear,' said Lizzie. 'This isn't what was meant to happen at all. Poor James! We'd better go and see if he's all right.'

Alex, leading the white horse - which would not now be carrying a damsel off into the sunset – went first and Lizzie followed him, and when they got there, Jane was already soothing a cursing James.

'What had she got in that reticule?' asked James, taking his hand away from his face to reveal a rapidly-developing black eye. 'It felt like an iron bar. She doesn't collect anvils by any chance, does she? I wouldn't put it past her, a girl like that's capable of anything. Did you see the way she stamped on my foot? It was vicious. And as for the way she swung her reticule . . . That girl's not a young lady, she's a confirmed bruiser. No wonder the burglars ran a mile.'

'Poor James!' said Jane sympathetically.

'Poor James my foot,' said Sophy. 'Trust you to make a mull of it, James. Just because she put up a bit of a fight.'

'A bit of a fight?' demanded James. 'She'd have given Gentleman Jackson a run for his money, and that's saying something, I can tell you. If Melody's ever short of money she can take a job there and give boxing lessons.'

'It looks like she collects pebbles,' said Alex, bending down to look at a few wet, shiny stones that were lying in the middle of the track. He picked them up and turned them over in his hand. 'These fell out of her reticule.'

'Pebbles!' said James. 'Those were no pebbles, they felt more like rocks.'

'That explains it,' said Lizzie, looking at the stones. 'I heard Melody talking about making a rockery when I was at the ball the other night. Her little sister wants to make one and Melody was offering to help her. She must have picked up the pebbles on the beach so that she could take them home for her sister.'

'You poor thing,' said Jane soothingly to James, ignoring Lizzie completely. 'Your eye's black and blue. We should never have come up with this scheme, it was a ridiculous idea in the first place, I said so all along.'

Lizzie looked at her in amazement and Sophy looked at her in disgust. Jane had never said any such thing!

'Putting James in danger was stupid,' said Jane, turning on them angrily. 'It could have got him killed.'

'Oh, for goodness sake, we weren't asking him to lead a cavalry charge against Napoleon,' said Sophy cuttingly. 'We were only expecting him to grab hold of a slip of a girl for a couple of minutes and then hang onto her until reinforcements arrived. It's typical of James that he couldn't even get such a simple thing right.' And with this cousinly aspersion on James's manly abilities she walked off in disgust.

'Take no notice of her,' said Jane helping James to his feet. 'It wasn't your fault. Melody Vauxhall's quite clearly a termagant, I'm just grateful the damage wasn't worse.'

'Oh, well, that's one idea that didn't work,' sighed Lizzie as she watched Jane leading James over to a fallen tree trunk, where she proceeded to examine his eye.

'Never mind. It was a good plan,' Alex reassured her. 'It isn't your fault it didn't work. It was just unlucky Melody had been down on the seashore collecting pebbles, it would have been completely different if she'd had wild flowers in her reticule instead.'

Lizzie laughed, whilst thinking, Goodness, it's usually me reassuring Alex, but now he's reassuring me.

It was a real change from their usual roles, and it was rather nice. It was sweet of him to cheer her up when her plan had gone badly wrong.

'I'd better take the horse back to the stables,' said Alex. 'He's not going to be needed any more, and as I hired him by the hour I want to get him back to the stable owner as quickly as possible.'

Lizzie nodded.

'I'm sorry,' she said. 'I really thought it would work. Perhaps we could try it again another day?'

He shook his head. 'There's no need. I know what I'm meant to do now, thanks to you, I didn't need to actually rescue Melody to get the idea. If Arabella's ever in need of any help, I'll now know I'm meant to sweep her off her feet and carry her indoors. A few weeks ago I might have been tempted to show her my watch!' he teased.

Lizzie chuckled, which was not surprising, as Alex had always had a way of making her see the funny side of things, and she was soon feeling much more cheerful.

'Good,' said Lizzie. 'You're right, you don't need any more practise. There's nothing more we can teach you, you make a wonderful rake. You know how to do everything except make conversation, and that will come, in time. The girls and I are leaving Kent on Saturday and we are going back to London. I expect we'll see you there.'

'Of course you will,' said Alex. 'I'm looking forward to it. It will give me a chance to put everything I've learnt to the test.'

He swung his leg over the back of his horse, and then giving her a final wave he rode back to the stables.

Once he had gone, the girls helped James back to the house. James took off his rough clothes in the gazebo and changed back into his normal clothes. Sophy and

Lizzie took the rough clothes back to the attic and James went into the drawing-room, with Jane following him. It was bad luck, but the butler was just coming out.

He took one look at James's black eye and they froze, wondering how they were going to explain it away. But luckily the butler guessed, quite wrongly, that James had been thrown from his horse, and he suggested some ice from the ice house to make the swelling go down. He soon came back with some ice in a muslin bag.

'Thank you,' said Jane, taking the ice.

The butler left the room, and Jane took the ice over to James as he lay on the sofa.

'Hold it to your face,' said Jane.

He did as she said.

'That was a rotten thing to happen,' she remarked.

'Oh, I don't know. It was nothing really,' said James.

Now that he was safely back home, and now that the first flush of pain had subsided, he was enjoying all the attention he was getting. Perhaps it wasn't so bad that he'd been hit with a reticule containing half of Kent's shoreline if it meant he was fussed over by Jane.

'I hope it won't stop you going up to London next week,' said Jane nonchalantly. 'Sophy says you were planning to go to town. It would be a shame if you had to put off your plans just because of this.'

'Don't worry. A little thing like this won't stop me. It's only a scratch,' he said manfully.

'It's a bit more than that,' said Jane. 'It was a

nasty blow. I don't know what Melody could have been thinking of. I knew she was a termagant, but I never expected her to do something like this.'

'Well, she did think I was a footpad,' said James.

'I suppose there is that,' Jane conceded. 'But your eye's going to be black and blue for quite a while.'

'It's a good thing Jarvis assumed I'd been thrown from my horse. It will save me inventing any other excuse. The one thing I can never possibly do is admit the truth. If anyone learns I was bested by a young lady I'll never hold up my head again.'

'You're not worried Melody will tell anyone?'

'No. As far as Melody knows she was attacked by a footpad, and that's all she can say. With luck no one will associate me with a disreputable character prowling the common. Although, perhaps it's a pity Jarvis thought I'd been thrown from my horse after all. If I'd had some time to think about it, I could have come up with a more romantic explanation for my black eye. If I had,' he said musingly, 'do you think all the young ladies would have started falling over me as they are falling over Alex?'

'No.' Jane took herself by surprise. She hadn't meant to sound so horrified. 'What I mean is, if that's what you want . . . ' she began, flustered.

He thought about it. 'Do you know? I don't think I do. It must be nice to begin with, being drooled over, but I wouldn't like it for very long. I have the feeling it would soon start to become a bit of a bore.'

He lifted the ice bag away from his face and resettled it more comfortably, then said nonchalantly, 'You're going to be in London for a while, I understand.'

'Yes.' Jane was equally nonchalant. 'I will be there with my family for the whole of the Season.'

'I will probably see something of you, then.'

'Yes. Very likely.'

He cleared his throat. 'Perhaps I could call on you?'

Jane whispered, 'That would be nice.'

Chapter Seventeen

'I can't think why Jane wants to stay behind and nurse James,' said Sophy, as she and Lizzie attended their final engagement in Kent that evening. It was a dinner party at a neighbour's house. 'I know this dinner party will probably be tedious — the Blenkinsops will go on about their time in India — but really, staying at home with James must be ten times worse.'

'Can't you really understand?' asked Lizzie. 'It's as plain as day. Jane's sweet on him.'

Sophy pursed her lips. 'I thought so too to begin with, but I don't believe it. Jane has far too much sense. Besides, she's one of the spinsterhood. Why would she want to leave us for a man? And, given that she did, why on earth would she choose James?'

'Because he isn't stuffy. He agreed to help us with Melody, even though it resulted in him getting hurt — '

'We couldn't foresee that,' protested Sophy.

'No. But we should have foreseen there might be difficulties.'

'Even so — '

'And he didn't blame us,' went on Lizzie. 'He could have kicked up a fuss and said we'd got him into this mess — which we had — but he didn't. He took it like a man.'

'That's true. But — '

'And he's trustworthy. He didn't tell your parents we'd invented the story about an outbreak of measles, and he didn't go running to them and telling them we were holding clandestine meetings with an obvious rake.'

'I should think not!' said Sophy.

'He could have done,' Lizzie pointed out. 'And he also kept Alex's secret. You saw the way he looked at Alex at the Assembly Rooms. He was green with envy. And yet he didn't give Alex away, once he knew the truth of the matter. He could have ruined Alex's credit with everyone in Kent. In fact, if he'd been a jealous type, he could have spread the word in London. But he didn't. He just knuckled down and helped.'

'You make him sound like a paragon of virtues,' said Sophy crossly.

'In a way, he is. It's just because you're his cousin that you haven't noticed before.'

That made Sophy stop and think. 'Yes, I think you're right. James has always been a good sort.' Her face fell. 'Oh dear. Do you think this means we're going to lose Jane from the spinsterhood?'

'I don't know.'

'Probably not,' said Sophy more cheerfully. 'I dare say it will all blow over. James is nice enough, but he's hardly the sort of man to make a girl go weak at the knees.'

'No. And that is rather nice,' said Lizzie dreamily.

Sophy looked at her in surprise. 'Have you met someone who's done that to you?'

'No,' she said rather too quickly, 'of course I haven't. I only meant it would be rather nice if it were to happen.'

'Good,' said Sophy, satisfied, 'because we've got the whole Season in front of us and I mean us all to enjoy it. Still, it's good that Jane decided to stay with James in one way, it freed my aunt so that she could come with us. If Jane hadn't stayed, my aunt would have done it and James would have hated that. He doesn't like his mother making a fuss of him, and as we owe him for helping us with Melody I'm glad Jane has spared him that.'

'It's a good thing your elderly Cousin Constance lives with you, so it isn't improper for Jane to have stayed behind with him,' Lizzie remarked.

'It is,' said Sophy.

'All in all, I'm glad this business is over and done with,' said Lizzie. 'One way or another it's been a strain.'

'Never mind, we're going back to London tomorrow,' said Sophy. 'I mean to enjoy the Season, and if I don't miss my guess, so do you.'

Chapter Eighteen

'You're back.' Lizzie's mother was delighted as she welcomed Lizzie back to their town house. 'Did you have a nice time with Sophy's aunt?'

'Yes, thank you,' said Lizzie. She felt rather guilty about having left her mother alone in London, but consoled herself with the fact that her mother wouldn't have been lonely as she had plenty of friends.

'You didn't use your parasol,' said her mother as she looked at Lizzie critically. 'I know it's only March, but you should have used it to protect your face anyway. The weather's been unseasonably warm, and the sun's been unusually hot. Your skin's as brown as a nut.'

'Nonsense,' said Lizzie. She glanced at her lightly bronzed reflection in the mirror and saw that her winter pallor had been removed. 'I'm hardly brown at all. Besides I didn't take a parasol, I had no idea I might need it at this time of year.'

'March can be sunny,' her mother said. 'You should know that by now. However, it's too late to worry about it so come in and tell me all about your trip.'

Lizzie told her mother about the visit to Kent, although she said nothing of Alex's transformation. That was something her mother had yet to see. Lizzie's courage failed her as she thought of what her mother would say when she saw their country neighbour in the guise of a rake. But then she consoled herself with the fact that what was done was done and that nothing could change it now.

'London's filling up nicely,' said her mother when Lizzie had finished. 'The Ullcasters and Portlands are here, and the Rochesters and Framptons are arriving tomorrow. We are going to Lord and Lady Ullcaster's ball next week, and we are going to Madame DuPris salon in the morning so that you can have a last fitting for your gown.' She hesitated then said casually, 'The Ullcaster's oldest son will be at their ball. He's a very nice boy, he's handsome and he has good manners. He would make a very good husband.' She looked at Lizzie seriously. 'I will tell you frankly, Lizzie. I have my eye on him for you.'

Lizzie sighed. 'I do wish you would give up on this matchmaking,' she said. 'Sophy and I have decided we are happy to remain spinsters.'

'And Jane?' asked her mother, noticing she had not mentioned her other friend.

'Jane, too.'

'You didn't mention her,' said her mother perceptively.

'Didn't I?'

'No, you didn't. You said "Sophy and I".'

'A slip of the tongue,' said Lizzie uncomfortably. 'I must just be tired from the journey. Of course I meant Jane as well.'

But her mother was not to be so easily put off. 'Has Jane met someone? Some nice young man who would make her happy?'

'No, of course not. Jane is just as happy being a spinster as we are. It is spinsters who have all the fun in life, after all. They don't have a husband telling them what they can and can't do. They can choose their own occupations, and can come and go as they please. I'm sure the Ullcaster's boy is very nice, but I suggest you don't get his hopes up as I've no intention of marrying him.'

'Really, Lizzie, I don't know what to do with you. It's all very well your enjoying being a spinster now. You are young, and still have your life ahead of you. But there will come a time when it won't be so much fun. I just don't want you to wake up one morning and realize that you've missed out in life, because by then it will be too late to do anything about it. Still,' she said, rising, 'I can't put an old head on young shoulders. You must make your own mistakes. Just remember you won't have many more Seasons, and after that if you change your mind about getting married it will be too late.'

'I shan't change my mind,' said Lizzie.

But even as she said it she had doubts. Was it because what her mother said was true? That she wouldn't have her choices in front of her for ever? No. It wasn't that. She wasn't going to marry for the sake of it, no matter how charming the Ullcaster's boy might be. But still, there was something.

She dismissed it. It was probably nothing. 'And now, mother, I'm tired and dirty after my long journey. I think I'll go to my room and change my gown before dinner.'

Chapter Nineteen

'So this is it,' said Alex. 'This is what it's all been for. Tonight I go to my first London ball as a rake.'

He, James and the girls had gathered in his London home and he was listening to their last minute advice. This was the night he had been waiting for, when Arabella would fall for his charms, and he wanted everything to be just right.

'Remember to scowl,' said Jane.

'And swagger,' said Sophy.

'And smile mockingly,' said Lizzie.

'And if all else fails, laugh sardonically and walk off,' said Sophy.

'I'll remember,' said Alex.

'Are you sure Arabella's going tonight?' asked James. 'It would be pointless to get yourself all ready if she's not going to show up.'

'Sure,' said Alex.

'I asked her aunt,' explained Sophy, 'and she said that, yes, Arabella would be there. So you see everything's all set.'

'Now all Alex has to do is sweep her off her feet,' said Jane encouragingly.

'We'll all be there cheering you on,' said Lizzie.

She stood up and, going over to him, brushed a small speck of dust from his tailcoat with her hand. Then she straightened his cravat.

'It's just a shame I won't be going,' said James to Alex. 'I'd like to see how you get on. But I can't go with a face like this. My eye still looks shocking, and

I don't want to go to the ball and frighten everyone half to death.'

'I won't be going either,' said Jane, not meeting Lizzie's eye as she said it.

'Oh?' asked Lizzie. 'Why not?'

'I thought I'd keep James company instead.'

Lizzie and Sophy exchanged glances.

It'll blow over, Sophy mouthed to Lizzie.

Lizzie nodded. Jane had always loved doctoring her dolls, and looking after James was no different now that he had a black eye. Once it was better Jane would most probably lose interest and come running back to the spinsterhood.

'Well, Lizzie and I will be there to cheer you on,' said Sophy. 'Wild horses wouldn't keep me away.'

'And talking of being there to cheer you on, it's time we went to get ready,' said Lizzie.

She stood up.

'I'd better be going too,' said James.

'I'll see you at the ball, then,' said Alex.

The four of them left, with James escorting them back home. They stopped at Jane's house first, then went on to Lizzie's.

'What do you think?' asked Sophy, as she and Lizzie were about to part. 'Do you think he'll do it?'

'Sweep Arabella off her feet?'

Sophy nodded.

'I'm not sure,' said Lizzie.

'Neither am I. But I hope he manages it.'

'Yes,' said Lizzie. 'So do I.'

'Come on, Sophy,' James interrupted them.

Sophy rolled her eyes. 'Oh, very well. I'll see you at the ball,' she said to Lizzie.

Lizzie nodded, then went into the imposing townhouse.

I hope I'm not coming down with a sore throat, she thought, as she took off her bonnet. When I said I hoped Alex managed to sweep Arabella off her feet, my voice sounded awfully hollow.

'At last.' Sophy nudged Lizzie as the clock struck eleven and Alex swaggered into the ballroom. It didn't have quite such an electrical effect as when he'd walked into the Assembly Rooms in Kent, this being London, which was used to seeing such things, but even so heads turned. Not least of them being Arabella's.

'It's working,' said Sophy. 'Arabella's turned to look at him. She's started to fan herself. She's going pink. They're all good signs.'

For some reason Lizzie didn't want to watch Alex making a conquest of Arabella and said, 'I think I'll go and get an ice.'

She wandered out of the ballroom and into the anteroom where refreshments were being served. It was very elegant, with a long row of gilded mirrors and three chandeliers. There was a white cloth on the table, and silver sparkling everywhere. She was just beginning to think it had been a good idea to retreat to the refreshment room when she caught sight of her mother, and her mother was deep in conversation with Mrs Ullcaster.

Oh, dear, she sighed inwardly. If it isn't one thing, it's another.

She was wondering whether she could slip out of the room unnoticed when her mother looked up and saw her.

'Ah, Lizzie, there you are. You remember Mrs Ullcaster, don't you?'

Lizzie said she did.

'And this is her son, Raymond.'

A tall young man had just joined them with two glasses of champagne. He handed them to Lizzie's mother and his own mother before turning to look at Lizzie. He was tall and handsome, with dark hair and brown eyes, but there was an irritated set to his features, as though he wasn't pleased to see her.

He likes this even less than I do, thought Lizzie.

But there was nothing for it. She would just have to grin and bear it.

'Say something, Raymond,' said Mrs Ullcaster, giving her recalcitrant son a nudge.

'How do you do, Miss Carstairs?' He spoke politely, but with the air of a man who wished he was a hundred miles away, at least.

'Very well, thank you, Mr Ullcaster,' returned Lizzie gravely. 'How do you do?'

'Very well,' he replied.

Whereupon the conversation petered out.

But the two mothers were not to be deterred.

'Have you seen the terrace, Miss Carstairs?' asked Mrs Ullcaster, turning to Lizzie. 'It really is very fine.'

'No,' Lizzie was forced to admit. 'I haven't.'

'Then you must let Raymond show it to you,' said Mrs Ullcaster. 'Raymond, Miss Carstairs would like to see the terrace. Raymond loves terraces, don't you, Raymond? You'd like nothing better than to show Miss Carstairs this fine example.'

Raymond gritted his teeth but was far too polite to refuse his mother. Instead he said, 'I'd be only too happy to do so, but I'm persuaded Miss Carstairs would find it boring. In my opinion it's a very ordinary terrace. And the night air is so treacherous. I wouldn't want Miss Carstairs to take cold.'

'Lizzie never takes cold,' said her mother promptly. 'And she is well wrapped up in her shawl. She likes of all things to be outside on a fine winter's night.'

'Besides, it will only be for a few minutes,' said Mrs Ullcaster, 'and afterwards you can fetch her a glass of punch to warm her up again.'

Lizzie felt her heart sink. Her mother was obviously determined, and Mrs Ullcaster was no less so. Between the two of them, they had made it impossible for him to refuse, and equally impossible for her to do so, either.

Raymond grimaced. He couldn't raise any more objections, however, without seeming a loose screw, so he bowed to the inevitable and offered Lizzie his arm, leading her out onto the terrace.

'You don't need to worry,' she said, once they were out of earshot of their mothers. 'I don't want to marry any more than you do. My mother wants to find me a husband, and has decided that you are the one. She has been singing your praises all day, as I imagine your mother has been singing mine, but I have no intention of marrying, and don't intend to be pushed into something I don't want to do.'

He laughed. The tension had broken. 'You're right. My mother's spent all day telling me about your many accomplishments. How you can play the piano divinely — '

Lizzie chuckled. 'I'm always hitting the wrong notes!'

'And how you sing like a nightingale — '

'With a sore throat!'

'And how you can speak several languages — '

'I can say "please" and "thank you" in French, and ask the way to the palace in Russian! I had a Russian governess for a few months,' she explained. 'Though why I should want to ask my way to the palace, in the unlikely event that I should find myself in Russia, I don't know!'

'My mother is convinced you would make a wonderful wife,' he said as they walked along the terrace, with a stiff breeze blowing.

'I would make a dreadful wife! I have no desire to say, "Yes, sir" "No, sir" "Three bags full, sir" for the rest of my life. No, I have decided I will never get married. I would much rather remain unwed.'

'Then you don't want to marry me?' he asked, sounding hopeful.

'Not at all.'

'Thank goodness. Not that I've anything against you personally. I'm sure you're a charming young woman — even if you can't sing, and play the piano, and do all the hundred and one things young ladies are meant to be able to do. But I just don't want to get married. You may think married women have a rotten time, but how about married men? They are bullied and henpecked all the time. "What time will you be in for dinner? Why are you going to the club? You never pay me any attention. You love that horse more than you love me". Oh, no, marriage is not for me.'

'Then we're agreed,' said Lizzie, as they turned at the end of the terrace and walked back again.

'We are. Which might be useful,' he said thoughtfully. 'If you've no objections, we can use this situation to our advantage.'

'How do you mean?' asked Lizzie.

'If we pretend to be interested in each other, then we might get a little peace. My mother won't rest until she's found me a wife, but if she thinks I'm courting you she'll leave me alone, at least for a while.'

'And my mother is determined to see me married before the end of the Season,' said Lizzie. 'But she won't find me any more eligible bachelors if she thinks I might marry you.' She pulled her shawl more tightly about her whilst she gave it her consideration. 'Yes, it could work.'

'We will only have to talk to each other companionably every time we see each other — ' he said.

'Dance a few dances — ' Lizzie added thoughtfully.

'And take a ride together in the park. I'll pay a few calls,' went on Raymond.

'And then they'll both be happy.'

'Which means that we can enjoy the Season in peace.'

'An excellent idea.'

'Then I suggest we begin. But first of all I'd better get you back in the warm. What my mother was thinking of I don't know. No sooner had she found me an eligible young lady than she tried to kill her off with pneumonia.'

'She must have been desperate,' smiled Lizzie. 'Viewing a terrace might be romantic at other times of year, but not in March.'

'And then, when I've found you something hot to drink, I hope I may have the pleasure of your hand for the next dance.'

'You may,' said Lizzie.

He gave her his arm and together they went into the ballroom.

To their mothers' delight, Raymond fetched Lizzie a glass of punch, and then they took their places on the dance floor for the waltz.

Chapter Twenty

Sophy watched Arabella go over to Alex with baited breath. He had made a wonderful entrance, but would he remember what to do? She saw Arabella go over to him, and saw Alex giving her a mocking smile. Good for him. He'd managed it. For whilst it was one thing to smile mockingly at someone he didn't know and didn't care about, it was another to manage it when he was smiling mockingly at a woman whose heart he hoped to win.

Well, then. So far so good.

Then Arabella said something.

From where she was standing, Sophy couldn't hear what it was, but she heard Alex's sardonic laughter, and saw him kissing Arabella's hand and walking off. Better and better! He was carrying off his part with aplomb!

Arabella's face was a picture. The petulant beauty, used to constant admiration, obviously couldn't understand what had gone wrong. She was so used to her blue eyes and golden curls working like a charm that she didn't know what to do when they didn't work any more.

Well done, Alex, thought Sophy. You've piqued Arabella's curiosity. She watched curiously to see what he would do next. He swaggered over to the other side of the room and Arabella hesitated for a few minutes, then followed him. It was all working out even better than they'd expected.

Sophy was just about to go and find Lizzie, and

tell her that everything was going to plan, when her attention was distracted. Wrexham had just walked into the room.

Sophy's heart skipped a beat. There was something about Wrexham. Of all the rakes he was the most handsome and the most unattainable, and she wouldn't have been a woman if she didn't find him heart stoppingly gorgeous. His dark hair fell carelessly onto his collar, and his sharply etched features held a hint of ruthlessness. His chin, rather than being clean shaven as was fashionable, was covered by dark stubble, giving him a devil-may-care look. His clothes fit him like a glove. His body was long and lean.

But even better than this, there was something else about Wrexham. It was a hint of something unfathomable in his eyes, a haunted look that no one else could achieve.

To her surprise, Sophy saw that he was looking at Alex. A strange expression crossed his face. Was he jealous? she wondered. But no, it couldn't be that. With looks like his, Wrexham need never be jealous of anyone. Besides, it wasn't a jealous expression. It was funny, but if she hadn't known better she'd have thought it was a look of pity.

How peculiar. Why should he feel sorry for Alex?

She didn't have time to think any more about it because, with one last look at Alex, he turned round and started walking straight towards her.

Her heart skipped a beat. But then she told herself not to be so silly. He must have seen someone glamorous behind her. A notable beauty like Miss

Hampton, perhaps, or a dazzling widow such as Mrs Tremaine. He might appear to be walking towards her, but at any minute he would walk past her, as Arabella had walked past Alex all those weeks ago, and walk into the arms of an acclaimed beauty.

She could bear it no longer. She looked round to see who he was making for, but there was no one behind her. Her heart began to beat faster and her legs turned to syllabub.

But even so, he was probably making for the card room or the refreshment room. Yes, that must be it.

But no, that wasn't it, because he was stopping in front of her with a strange look on his face.

'I know what you're doing,' he said.

She couldn't quite take it in. Lord Wrexham was talking to her. Her! Sophy Lyndhurst! The world's most desirable rake was standing in front of her and talking to her. It didn't make sense of course, what he was saying, but what did that matter? She couldn't have everything.

'You're making a big mistake.' His eyes burned into her and she felt most peculiar. Her heart was beating so loudly she was sure he must hear it, and her cheeks felt as though they were about to burst into flame.

She knew what she should do. She ought to smile knowingly and tap him with her fan, but instead her honesty got the better of her and she said, 'I don't know what you're talking about.'

Oh, no! she thought in despair as she heard herself. You're talking to the most handsome rake in London and all you can say is, "I don't know what you're talking about!" You're as bad as Alex.

But Wrexham hadn't finished with her. Instead of smiling mockingly and walking off, making her feel three inches tall for making such an absurd remark, he said, 'You're turning him into a rake.'

Goodness! So that was what he was talking about! He knew what they were doing with Alex. And by his expression, he thought it was a mistake. Was it because he didn't want the competition? No. With the best will in the world no one could think of Alex as competition. And certainly not Wrexham who had had women falling at his feet for years. It must be something else.

'It won't make him happy,' he said. His eyes were haunted. 'Being a rake's the loneliest thing in the world.'

And then he walked off. Just like that. Leaving Sophy reeling.

What was he talking about, being a rake's the loneliest thing in the world? she wondered. She didn't know. But she'd never get a chance to ask, because he'd never condescend to talk to her again.

Still, he'd talked to her once and that was more than most people could say. Now she really must find Lizzie, because she couldn't wait to tell her all about it.

Chapter Twenty-One

Where is Lizzie? thought Alex.

He should have been keeping his mind on what he was doing but for some reason he couldn't concentrate, even though the evening had started well. To begin with, he'd been really pleased with things. Arabella had looked up at his entrance, and he'd been able to tell by her parted lips and wide eyes that she was attracted to him.

So far, so good.

Then things had got even better, as she had walked over to him and started flirting with him. It had felt so good, to know that this time she had walked across the room to see him, and not to see Wrexham. A fact made even more pointed when soon afterwards Wrexham himself had entered the room and Arabella hadn't even noticed.

Better still, he hadn't made a fool of himself. All the practise he'd had in Kent had paid off. He hadn't said anything ridiculous. Instead, he'd kept his calm, letting her talk herself into an embarrassed silence before giving her a mocking smile and walking off.

To his amazement, it had done the trick. Instead of being disgusted with his bad behaviour she'd followed him with her eyes and then, drawn to him like a moth to a flame, she'd followed him with the rest of her. She simply couldn't get enough of him. But he was in danger of ruining it all because he couldn't keep his mind off Lizzie.

Why he was so concerned about Lizzie he didn't

know. But he was. It had started when he'd seen her go into the anteroom where refreshments were being served. That in itself had surprised him because he had thought she would be keeping an eye on his progress. And then her mother had introducing her to someone, and his discomfort had increased, because it was to Ullcaster. One of the handsomest and most eligible men in the room.

He had expected her to acknowledge the introduction and then have something to eat, or a glass of champagne, perhaps, to drink, before returning to the ballroom. But instead she had stayed in the refreshment room, and was busy talking to Ullcaster.

Ullcaster, he thought in disgust. Ullcaster wouldn't do for her. The man was too fond of horses and drink. If Lizzie married him she'd never see him. He wouldn't want to spend his time in the country, he'd want to live in town. And when in town he'd always be at his club. That kind of life wouldn't satisfy Lizzie. She'd want a husband she could see, especially once she had children. It would be no good to her if her husband was out drinking all night and carousing with his friends, not returning home until the early hours of the morning. She'd want him on the family estate, playing with the children, teaching them how to ride a pony and making sure they could swim.

Arabella was saying something.

'I didn't know what you were really like when I met you before,' she was saying coyly. 'I thought you must be boring, but I realize now that was just a pose. It was a good idea. It kept all the girls away from you.

You must get so tired of being pursued.' She gave him a languishing look with her big blue eyes and flirted expertly with her fan.

Instead of replying sensibly he gave her a sardonic smile which pleased her no end, leaving him free to think about Lizzie. What was she doing now? She was going out onto the terrace with Ullcaster. His brow darkened. What was he doing taking her outside in this weather? Didn't he know it was March? And what was her mother thinking of? She should be preventing it, instead of looking on and smiling. And as if that wasn't bad enough, Ullcaster's mother was smiling too.

So that was it. They'd planned it between them, and Lizzie was caught in their web. Thank goodness there were other people out on the terrace - hardy or foolish, he didn't know which - so that at least she wouldn't be compromised. Even so, he had a good mind to follow her and tell her she was making a big mistake. If she wasn't careful her mother would marry her off to Ullcaster, and then where would she be?

'I would so love to waltz.'

Arabella's remark brought him back to reality. It was none of his business what Lizzie did, after all, and here was Arabella all but falling into his arms. Her white bosom was rising and falling in the most alluring way and he tried not to look at it, because he was finding it difficult enough to think without that added distraction. He wanted to dance with her but he couldn't help thinking that if he fell in with her wishes she'd no longer see him as a rake, but as her lapdog instead.

What to do? Be a rake and lose his chance to dance with the woman he had longed to hold in his arms for months? Or become her lapdog and risk having her never wanting to dance with him again?

He made his decision. Being a rake had worked wonders so far. He'd just have to pray it would work again. Letting his gaze roam over her body, he undressed her with his eyes. He was by now very good at it and he had the satisfaction of seeing her blush to the roots of her hair. He gave her a mocking smile. Then he said, 'In that case I mustn't detain you,' and taking her hand, he gave it a long, lingering kiss, before making her a bow and walking away from her.

In the gilded mirror to the side of him he caught sight of Arabella's startled reaction. And then saw a look of longing spread over her face. Lord, what fools these women be, he thought contemptuously, giving a twist to Shakespeare, for if that was all it took to make women swoon over him then it was easier than shooting fish in a barrel. And shooting fish in a barrel had never interested him.

Thank goodness Lizzie isn't taken in by such foolishness, he thought with relief. At least there is one woman in all England who has a brain in her head.

At least, he'd always thought so, but seeing her come back into the ballroom and take to the floor with Ullcaster he suddenly wasn't so sure.

Chapter Twenty-Two

'You really don't have to play chess with me,' said James as Jane, complete with her mother and father, kept him company by having dinner with him that evening. 'I know young ladies don't like chess. Sophy hates it. So why not talk to me instead?'

'You're wrong. I don't hate it,' said Jane, setting out the pieces whilst her parents talked to James's parents. 'I like chess, I've been playing since I was a little girl.'

'The bishop goes there,' said James, pointing to one of the squares as she took the bishop out of the wooden box. 'The bishop's the one with the pointed top.'

'I know which one the bishop is,' said Jane with an amused smile. Really, did he think she'd never played chess before? If so, he was in for a big surprise.

'Good for you,' said James. 'And the knight - that's the one that looks like a horse - goes over there.'

'The one that looks like a horse,' said Jane, pretending to frown. If he insisted on treating her like a numbskull, then he deserved his come-uppance. She may be fond of James, but she had no intention of letting him get away with it. 'Ah, yes. This must be it.' She gave him a sideways glance as she picked up the queen.

'No. It's this one,' he said, handing her the knight.

'Oh, yes, of course. How silly of me!' She smiled sweetly, and remarked teasingly, 'It's very kind of you to help me out like this.'

'That's all right. It's only chivalrous, you know. If you insist on playing, then we'll play, but I don't want to take advantage of you — '

'What with me being a poor, helpless female,' interposed Jane innocently.

James flashed her a suspicious glance, and she realized she had gone too far. She quickly retreated, saying, 'Even so, I'd like to make it more interesting. What do you say we stake a wager on the outcome of the game?'

'A wager?' He threw up his hands in horror. 'I couldn't do that. It would be like taking a rattle from a baby.'

'Say, five guineas?' asked Jane. She had found his attitude amusing to begin with, but now it was beginning to rouse her fighting spirit. Like taking a rattle from a baby indeed!

'I couldn't possibly — '

She looked at him enquiringly.

'Oh, very well,' he said.

'Good.' Jane became business like. She finished setting out the pieces and then said, 'Let's begin.'

Alex leant over the chess board. 'You go first. Just move one of the — oh, I see, you've already done it. You've moved the queen's pawn.'

He settled down to his own move and they began in earnest. As the game progressed his face began to lose the tolerant look it had worn earlier, and became a picture of concentration as he tried to outplay her.

'Check,' said Jane half an hour later as she took

yet another of James's pieces, this time a castle.

'Not again.'

He sounded bewildered, and Jane gave a mischievous smile. He'd assumed she was having a run of beginner's luck at the start of the game, but he was at last being forced to realize that when she'd said she was good at chess it was not an idle boast.

'You'd better move your queen,' she said helpfully. 'otherwise — '

'I don't need you telling me what to do.' He frowned. 'I'll decide on my next move myself.' His fingers hovered over his remaining castle, but then he moved his bishop.

Jane gave a silvery laugh. 'Check mate,' she said as she removed his queen.

'Oh, no! I didn't see it coming. Where did you learn to play chess like that?'

'At my father's knee,' she said.

'I owe you five guineas.'

'Don't worry. I won't let you pay. I was just cross because you thought I wasn't going to be any good. I did try and tell you, but you wouldn't listen.'

'That's because I've never seen a young lady play chess like that before. But I insist on settling our wager. A gentleman always pays his debts.' He became suddenly bashful. 'Perhaps I could settle it by taking you to Gunter's for an ice?'

'I'd like that,' said Jane nonchalantly.

'Tomorrow?' asked James.

Jane hesitated. She didn't know what the girls were doing tomorrow, and besides she wanted to know what had happened to Alex at the ball. But she could always find out in the morning, and then go to

Gunter's in the afternoon.

'That's a good idea,' she said.

'Then it's settled.'

'Have you two finished your game yet?' asked James's father.

'Yes. Jane beat me,' James admitted.

'My word.' James's father looked at her with respect. 'Good for you.'

Jane's father laughed. 'It's a brave man who'll play Jane at chess. She beats me every time.'

But her mother admonished her on their way home in the carriage. 'You should have let him win, my dear,' she said. 'Gentlemen don't like to be beaten. Especially at something like chess.'

'Pish,' said her father. 'Don't you go hiding your lights under a bushel, Janey. That James of yours is a nice young man. He won't object to a clever wife.'

'Really, Papa,' said Jane flustered. 'I don't know what you mean.'

'Well, I won't tease you any more. But I think I'll order a new waistcoat all the same. I'll want to look my best when I walk you down the aisle.'

Chapter Twenty-Three

Sophy was feeling pensive the following morning. Try as she might she couldn't forget her strange conversation with Wrexham the evening before. What did he mean by saying a rake was the loneliest person in the world? She couldn't understand it. And she couldn't understand him. There was definitely more to Wrexham than met the eye.

She decided to go for a ride. The morning was fine, and with any luck the exercise would drive the conversation out of her mind. Donning a fetching riding habit she took her horse into Hyde Park. Her groom, who always accompanied her on her rides, followed her at a short distance behind.

There were not many other people riding in the park. Both the Ladies' Mile and Rotten Row were choc-a-bloc in the Season, but at this time of year it was often almost empty, particularly on days like today when the weather was not very nice. But there was one other rider in the park, and Sophy recognised him at once. It was Wrexham. He was exercising his coal-black horse.

'Miss Lyndhurst,' he said, tipping his hat to her as she cleared the Ladies' Mile and drew level with him.

'Lord Wrexham,' she acknowledged him. Then, impulsively, she reined in her horse and said, 'What did you mean last night, when you said that being a rake's the loneliest thing in the world? I've thought about it all night and I can't understand it. Surely it must be the least lonely? After all, you can have any woman you want.'

She should have been embarrassed to be talking about such things, but somehow she wasn't. She felt comfortable with Wrexham, though she couldn't think why. Perhaps it was because he had talked to her the evening before, really talked to her, not just making light conversation or indulging in flirtation, but as though he'd had something important to say.

He reined in his own horse and rested his arms on the pommel of his saddle.

She couldn't help it, her heart began to beat faster. He was looking wickedly handsome. His face was unshaven and a shadow of dark stubble was visible around his mouth. And what a mouth! It was full and sensuous, and yet sensitive at the same time. No wonder women dreamt about him! But there was something more, she thought, puzzled. It was something she hadn't noticed before, something in his eyes. Not just the haunted look she'd seen earlier. It was more than that. It was as though a glimpse of his soul was shining out of their dark depths.

She shivered, and he gave a wicked smile. But she forced herself to concentrate and said, 'What did you mean?'

She saw the glimpse of his soul disappear as the mocking smile curled his lip. She had the sudden feeling he was about to say something sardonic. She thought of Alex, and all they'd taught him, how rakes were sardonic when they wanted to get out of a difficult situation. Without thinking what she was doing she put her hand out and touched his arm to stop him.

'No, don't do that. I really want to know. Why is being a rake such a lonely thing to be when you can have any woman under the sun?'

The mocking smile left his lips. He looked at her long and deeply, then said, 'I can have any woman under the sun . . . as long as she's of a certain type.'

'A certain type?' asked Sophy, puzzled again. 'Unmarried, do you mean?'

He threw her another wicked smile. 'No, that's not what I mean. Unmarried or married makes no difference. Nor does young or old, rich or poor. But she has to be the type who's taken in by appearances, and who is easily impressed. And most importantly she has to be someone who doesn't care about reputation.'

'Hers or yours?' asked Sophy, chewing her bottom lip with a frown.

'Both,' he said. 'But I was thinking of mine.'

'But why does that matter? It still gives you plenty of women to mix with.'

'But not the ones I want to mix with. Not any I could respect. I've run up huge debts in the last few years — not as bad as is generally believed, but bad enough. I have a large mortgage on my estate. I drink. I gamble. I've had a string of mistresses and as many affairs. And women find it attractive . . . ' He shook his head in disgust. 'Or at least, the wrong kind of women do. The right kind . . . ' He shrugged. Then suddenly he became sardonic again. 'But I've said enough,' he remarked. And flashing her a mocking smile, he tipped his hat and rode away.

Stranger and stranger, thought Sophy with a puzzled air as she watched him ride off.

Her groom, finally catching her up, joined her. His horse was not as fleet—footed as hers, and he had lagged behind.

She set off again. Wrexham was turning out to be a very complex man. Perhaps she'd underestimated rakes. Perhaps there was more to all of them than met the eye. Or perhaps Wrexham was unusual even for a rake.

Really, she'd come on this ride to try and get rid of her perplexed feelings, but instead they'd just become ten times worse.

Chapter Twenty-Four

Lizzie was holding open house. It was the morning after the ball, and Jane, Sophy and Alex had congregated in her drawing room. Miss Withershanks, carrying out her duty as a chaperon, was settled at the far side of the room with a fashion journal, leaving the girls and Alex free to talk.

'So tell me. I'm dying to know all about it,' said Jane. 'How did it go?'

'Brilliantly,' said Alex. 'Arabella was smitten. She followed me round the room, and by the end of the evening I had her eating out of my hand. There is just one problem.'

'Yes?' asked Lizzie.

'How am I ever going to dance with her if I have to go on behaving like a rake?'

He had already told them of Arabella's hint that she would like to waltz the previous evening, and his own mocking reply, but he was still puzzling over the problem of how he was ever to take her into his arms without appearing to be a lap dog.

'That's easy,' said Jane. 'Take her onto the terrace and dance with her there.'

'Speaking of terraces, what were you doing on the terrace with Ullcaster last night?' asked Alex.

'You were on the terrace with Ullcaster?' asked Sophy in surprise. 'I didn't see that.'

'Goodness,' said Jane. 'What on earth were you doing with Ullcaster?'

Lizzie hesitated. If she told them about her

arrangement with Ullcaster they were bound to let something slip out, and then her mother would know what she was doing. And once her mother found out that her interest in Ullcaster was a pretence, then she would start introducing her to other eligible bachelors straight away.

'Looking at the stars,' she said.

'Looking at the stars?' asked Sophy.

'They are very interesting,' said Lizzie awkwardly. For some reason Alex's eyes were on her, and he wasn't looking pleased.

'Whatever next? Although it does sound rather nice,' Jane said thoughtfully.

'Yes, I think that's a good idea,' said Alex. 'The next time I'm at a ball I'll take Arabella onto the terrace.'

'It might be raining,' said Lizzie hastily.

'Then I'll take her into the conservatory, and we'll waltz between the plants. If I whisk her in there when she least expects it, and leave her high and dry at the end of it, I should be able to dance with her without her losing interest in me.'

No! Lizzie wanted to cry out. That's not a good idea at all!

The thought of Alex waltzing with Arabella in the conservatory was horrible.

But of course she didn't cry out. She couldn't. It would seem strange.

'That's a good idea,' said Sophy. Then she hesitated. She looked as though she was about to say something important. 'You do like Arabella, don't you?' she asked. 'She's not the wrong sort?'

'No, of course not. She's wonderful. I don't know

what you mean,' said Alex, although he didn't sound quite convinced.

'What made you ask that?' asked Jane curiously.

'Oh, nothing. It's just that I wondered, that's all. What I mean to say is, I wondered if being a rake is all it's made out to be. If you were enjoying it, or if it's turned out to be a big mistake.'

'No. I like it,' said Alex firmly.

'That's good.' But Sophy didn't sound certain.

'Well, of course he likes it,' said Jane in exasperation. 'Otherwise he wouldn't have wanted us to help him in the first place.'

'I suppose so,' Sophy admitted. 'Well, I'm glad you had a good evening, Alex. Now tell us, Jane, how did your evening go?'

Jane went slightly pink. 'Very well,' she said. Then she grinned mischievously. 'I beat James at chess!'

Sophy laughed. 'I bet he didn't know how good you were.'

'No. He didn't. He thought I didn't know how to play. So I decided to teach him a lesson.'

'A wager?' asked Lizzie, joining in the conversation once again.

Jane nodded. 'Five guineas.'

'He lost, of course,' said Sophy. 'James has never been very good at chess.'

'He did,' agreed Jane. 'I told him he needn't pay it, but he insisted a gentleman always paid his debts, so he's taking me to Gunter's for an ice this afternoon by way of settling his account.'

Sophy and Lizzie both gave her curious glances, and she went even more pink.

Fortunately, Alex was less curious, and saved her by asking Sophy, 'How was your ride?'

She started. 'My ride? How do you know I went out for a ride?'

'I saw you in Hyde Park. I went out myself.' He looked down at his hard, sleek body. 'I have to keep myself mean and lean.'

'Of course.' Sophy's smile was half-hearted. 'Did you . . . did you happen to see who I was with?' she asked casually.

'No, should I have?'

'No, of course not,' she said, flustered.

'Who were you with?' asked Jane curiously.

'My groom, of course.'

Now it was Sophy's turn to be looked at curiously by the other two girls. She maintained her calm. All the same, she thanked her lucky stars that she hadn't been seen with Wrexham. She'd only been talking with him, but even that would have been enough to cast a doubt on her reputation.

Fortunately for her peace of mind, the other two girls then turned their attention back to Alex.

'So tell me,' said Jane, as she pulled her legs up beneath her and settled herself more comfortably on the chaise longue, 'What do you intend to do with Arabella once you've caught her? Do you mean to marry her?'

Alex looked startled. 'I don't know. I hadn't really thought about it. Yes, I suppose so,' he said cautiously. Then frowned.

'I only ask because her father won't like it,' said Jane. 'Not with you looking the way you do. It's one thing for young ladies to drool over rakes, but for their fathers to take to them is quite another. If you do decide to marry her, you'd better not go and ask for her hand looking like that. If you do, her father will probably drive you off his land.'

'Oh, well, that's a long way off,' said Alex evasively. 'I haven't even danced with her yet. There's no point in thinking about asking her to marry me until I know she'll say yes. And once that's happened, it will be soon enough to worry about her parents.'

Jane said, 'That's very true. Well, I must be going. I'm having lunch early so that I won't be too full to eat an ice at Gunter's this afternoon. Are you going to Lady Halverston's soirée on Friday?'

Lizzie nodded.

Alex said, 'So am I.'

'Me too,' sighed Sophy. 'If there's one thing I can't abide it's a soirée, but mother's already accepted the invitation so I have to go.'

'I know what you mean. They're not my favourite sort of entertainment either. But at least if there's music it will mean Alex will have a chance to persuade Arabella to dance.'

'That's true,' said Sophy.

'And now I must go.'

Jane left them, and a few minutes later, Sophy said, 'I'd better go, too.'

'Well,' said Alex awkwardly, when she had gone.

'Well,' said Lizzie.

'About Ullcaster . . . ' said Alex.

Lizzie looked surprised.

'Yes?' she asked.

He looked as though he was about to speak. But

then changed his mind.

    'Oh, nothing,' he said. 'I'll see you at the soirée.'

Chapter Twenty-Five

'Lizzie, you have a visitor.' Lizzie's mother bustled importantly into her bedroom the next morning. 'Raymond Ullcaster's paid a call. Put on your blue silk, tidy your hair quickly, and then come downstairs.'

'Don't worry, mother, Mr Ullcaster won't care what dress I'm wearing,' said Lizzie. Biting her tongue a moment later, for it was not what she had meant to say.

'Don't be so silly,' said her mother. 'Of course he will. Really, Lizzie, sometimes I despair of you. Now, look lively. Slip into your blue gown and I'll send Talbot along to help you with your hair.'

Lizzie gave in. It looked as though she was going to have to make herself presentable, even though what she had said was true: Raymond Ullcaster wouldn't care one way or another what she wore. But it would be worth it if it helped to pull the wool over her mother's eyes.

Besides, whatever her own feelings, she owed it to Raymond to carry on with the pretence. They had agreed to show some interest in each other in order to protect themselves from the machinations of their matchmaking mothers, and she could not now go back on her side of the bargain.

Twenty minutes later she was dressed in her best blue silk. It was a lovely gown, its high waist ornamented by a strip of satin ribbon and its puffed sleeves decorated with a row of frills. She tripped into the drawing-room and greeted Raymond with her best smile.

'Mr Ullcaster. How nice to see you. Do sit down.'

Her mother, who had been keeping Raymond amused until Lizzie should appear, smiled indulgently at Lizzie's impeccable manners. Lizzie felt a twinge of guilt at her mother's obvious happiness. She didn't like deceiving her mother. But at the same time, she knew that if she didn't do it, her mother would give her no peace.

'It's good of you to receive me.' Raymond, too, was on his best behaviour, and was being at his most charming. 'I hope you enjoyed the ball the other night?'

'Yes, thank you. It was most agreeable.'

There was an unfortunate silence whilst both Lizzie and Raymond cast about for something to say. But Mrs Carstairs was not about to let it continue.

'Lizzie, show Lord Ullcaster your sketchbook,' she said. She turned to Raymond. 'Lizzie does the most wonderful sketches. She's a very gifted artist. Really, a most talented girl.'

'I'm sure she's very accomplished,' he said, but there was a twinkle in his eye.

'Oh, yes she is,' agreed her mother, much to Lizzie's embarrassment. 'She sings divinely, and plays the piano in the most wonderful — '

'Here,' said Lizzie, hurriedly opening her sketchbook, which was conveniently close to hand. Ordinarily she shrank from showing her artistic endeavours to anyone, but she was terrified that if she didn't do so immediately, then her mother would ask her to sing, and that would be far worse. 'This is my sketchbook.'

'Oh, yes. That's an excellent hound,' said Raymond as he opened the sketchbook at the first page.

'You're mistaken, Mr Ullcaster,' said Lizzie's mother firmly, 'that is Lizzie's horse.'

'Of course it is,' he said. To his credit, he managed not to laugh. 'That is what I meant to say.'

'Do you ride, Mr Ullcaster?' asked Lizzie's mother.

'Yes, I do.'

'I'm glad to hear it. Fresh air and exercise are so important, particularly when one is in town. Lizzie rides every morning in Hyde Park. She likes a gallop along the Ladies' Mile. She is always to be found there at eleven o'clock. It is quite a ritual with her, but one I am glad to encourage, particularly as she rides so well.'

Lizzie looked astonished, as she had never been riding in Hyde Park in her life. But she quickly realized what was behind her mother's statement, and knew it wouldn't do for her to contradict. Besides, it wouldn't have done any good. Her mother was clearly determined that she and Raymond would bump into each other in the park, and with a sinking feeling she realized she would have to ride in the Row every morning from now on so that it could be accomplished.

Ah, well, there were worse ways of spending her mornings, after all, and at least he would be spared the necessity of calling on her every day as he could meet her in the park instead.

'Then perhaps I will see her there,' he said,

taking the hint. 'I certainly hope so. But now, I must take up no more of your time.' He stood up. 'It was good of you to receive me.'

'Not at all. It was good of you to call. We hope to see you again.'

He gave a courteous smile, and then took his leave of them.

'What a lovely man. No wonder Mrs Ullcaster is so proud of him,' said Lizzie's mother with satisfaction. 'Any woman would be glad to call him "son". Yes, he is a perfect gentleman. Do you not think so, Lizzie?'

'Oh, yes, certainly, mother,' said Lizzie dutifully.

'Good.' Mrs Carstairs smiled indulgently. 'Well, now, you had better go and change your dress. It will not do to get it dirty. And once you have changed into your muslin you may practise the piano. Then you can sing for Mr Ullcaster the next time he comes to call.'

Chapter Twenty-Six

Jane was looking forward to her visit to Gunter's, which was a favourite place of hers. The famous shop sold a mouth-watering selection of pastries and ices, and she often visited it when she was in London.

Dressed in a becoming sprigged muslin gown and wearing her prettiest bonnet she set out for her appointment with James. The carriage bowled through the London streets at a spanking pace, weaving its way through carts and carriages, negotiating bends and corners, until at last it came to Berkeley Square.

Goodness, it's busy, thought Jane, for the confectioner's was a popular one and there were a lot of other carriages parked around the square.

Her own carriage rolled to a halt. Sure enough there was James, leaning against the railings with a collection of other young men. He straightened up on seeing her and went over to her carriage.

'What would you like?' he asked her, when they had exchanged greetings. 'Remember, it must be something extravagant. You beat me at chess fair and square, and I want to make good on my wager.'

'I'm not sure,' she said, thinking of all the delicious things on offer. 'I can't decide. I think I will get out of the carriage and come with you.' Although young ladies generally stayed in their carriages and allowed themselves to be waited on by the gentlemen of their party, or, if there were no gentlemen, by Gunter's waiters, Jane wanted to stretch her legs.

'Very well,' he said. He handed her out of the carriage and escorted her over to the east side of the square where the shop stood. It was an attractive building. It had a sign with a pineapple on it hanging outside, to tell the world that it was indeed a confectioner's. 'Would you like an ice or a sorbet?' he asked her. 'Or perhaps you would prefer a pastry?'

'No. I think I'll have a sorbet.'

He ordered her the sorbet, and an ice for himself, and they returned to Jane's carriage where, chaperoned by her maid, they ate the delectable confections.

'And now, would you care to take a turn around the square?' James asked.

The afternoon was fine, if blustery, and Jane agreed.

'Do you think you will ever get married?' James surprised her by saying, as they walked past the window of Gunter's, in which a multi-tiered wedding cake was displayed.

'I don't know, I'm sure,' she said.

She was flustered by his question and didn't really know how to respond. A few weeks ago she would have laughed and said, "Marriage isn't for me". But now she was not so sure. It was true she enjoyed the single life, but she had begun to wonder whether there might be further pleasures to be had from marrying.

If a woman married a bully, she lost control of her life for sure, but if she married a man she liked and respected then she could still do much as she pleased. And she also had the pleasure of his company. Together with the pleasure of his kisses.

It was something that Jane hadn't thought about in recent years, but lately she had begun to wonder what it might feel like. She was about to ask when she realized she couldn't possibly enquire of James what it felt like to kiss someone. It would ruin her reputation to talk about such things. And besides, he would think she was fast. But she was curious all the same.

'Yes?' he asked, seeing she was about to speak.
'Oh, nothing,' she said. She went slightly pink.
'Jane . . . '
'Yes?'
'I was wondering . . .'
'Yes, James?'
'I was wondering if I could . . . oh, never mind.'

She had the feeling he'd been about to say something important, but had then changed his mind. It was a pity. She would have liked to know what he had been going to say.

It seemed that neither of them could speak their minds today. Which was odd, because she usually felt at ease with James.

'Will you be going to Lady Halverstone's on Friday?' he asked.

'Yes.'

'Good. My eye has healed, and I, too, will be there.'

She turned and looked at his face, searching for any trace of bruising that might remain. But fortunately it had at last disappeared.

'May I sit next to you?' he asked. 'At the soirée?'

Jane went pink again. 'Yes. You may. Although you may have to fight for your seat with Lizzie and

Sophy,' she teased him. 'They, too, will be there.'

'Lizzie will be too engrossed with Alex to fight me for a seat,' said James. 'And as for Sophy . . . ' he paused. 'Has she said anything to you?'

Jane was intrigued. 'What about?'

'Oh, nothing important. It was just an idea I'd had, that was all. But it was probably wide of the mark.'

By now they had walked round the square, and returned to Jane's carriage.

'Thank you for the sorbet,' she said.

He took her hand and kissed it. 'The pleasure was all mine.'

He helped her back into the carriage.

'I will see you at Lady Halverstone's, then,' he said.

Jane smiled, then bid him goodbye.

Chapter Twenty-Seven

Tonight's the night, thought Alex as he pulled on his tightly-fitting coat and fluffed out the lace of his shirt at the cuff. He had it all planned out. When the music started he was going to take Arabella into the conservatory and dance with her. He was going to be at his most rakish. He was going to make Arabella long for him to kiss her. And then he was going to walk off, leaving her longing for more.

A few weeks ago he would have been horrified at the idea of taking a young lady into the conservatory and making her want him to kiss her, but he was getting used to being a rake. And besides, he was getting results. Arabella hadn't looked at him twice when he'd been a country gentleman, but now that he was a swaggering rake she couldn't get enough of him. It wouldn't be long before he'd have conquered her heart. And then he'd make her his wife.

To begin with it hadn't seemed possible, but now he knew that anything was possible, even persuading her parents to agree to the match. And if they refused, why, by the time he'd finished with Arabella, she'd run off with him to Gretna Green!

Feeling very pleased with himself, he ran his fingers through his hair to give it an added touch of wildness and had a glass of brandy before he left the house. Rakes always smelt of brandy, and he had found a number of ways to give himself the authentic smell without having to drink too much of it. The most effective way was to pour a bit on his handkerchief so that he would still smell of it when he arrived at the soirée, without having to go to all the trouble of getting drunk. Besides, he'd need his wits about him this evening. He didn't want to spoil everything by falling over in the middle of the waltz.

Lizzie, too, was getting ready for the soirée.

'Now remember,' her mother said, 'be nice to Mr Ullcaster. Not too nice, mind. You don't want him to think you're too eager. That never does. It puts men off.'

'I'll remember,' said Lizzie.

'In fact,' said her mother thoughtfully, 'it won't hurt to make him a little jealous. Flirt a little with some of the other young gentlemen. Chatter engagingly with them, particularly if they're eligible. And don't forget, play with your fan. A fan is one of a woman's best weapons. It's attractive and alluring, and yet at the same time not too obvious.'

Lizzie resigned herself to listening to her mother's advice, although it couldn't have been more misplaced.

'And when you sit next to him, make sure you sit at his left. That way he'll see your best profile. The other one is not quite as attractive. And who knows,' she added, 'if you play your cards right, he might even make you an offer tonight.'

Lizzie felt rather guilty. 'I'll do everything you say, Mother, but don't get your hopes up. I don't believe he's serious in his intentions.' She felt she ought to give her mother a hint as to the true state of affairs.

'Nonsense, Lizzie. Of course he's serious. And,

more to the point, his mother is serious, too. She wants to see him make an eligible match as soon as possible. She is ready for him to start filling his nurseries and providing her with some much-wanted grandchildren, and as she holds the purse strings he will do as she says.'

Lizzie's face fell. She hadn't realized how deeply involved her mother and Mrs Ullcaster had become in their schemes. But it wasn't her fault if they chose to spend their time matchmaking when they hadn't been asked to do so.

'Now, Lizzie, don't look like that,' said her mother, misunderstanding the reasons for her expression. 'You love children as much as I do. And believe me, there is nothing better than having some of your own.'

'Perhaps. In time. But I still think you're wrong about Mr Ullcaster.'

'Well, if I am - although I can assure you I'm not - but if I am, then it will be an even better idea for you to flirt a little with some of the other gentlemen here tonight. They will give you something to fall back on if Mr Ullcaster doesn't come up to scratch.'

Lizzie could say no more. She put on her pearl earrings and her matching pearl necklace and then she was ready to go.

She and her mother set out and before long they found themselves at their destination. The carriage rolled to a halt and they went inside. Raymond Ullcaster was there right on cue, bowing over her hand and taking her to one side for a supposedly intimate conversation.

'It's working like a charm,' he said. 'My mother

hasn't introduced me to anyone else since I paid a call on you. She's convinced it's serious. Now all we have to do is keep it up until the end of the Season. It shouldn't be difficult. I just have to monopolise you tonight — '

Lizzie shook her head. 'You can't do that. Or rather, I can't let you. My mother's given me strict instructions to make you jealous, which means I have to laugh and flirt with other young men as well.'

'And that's supposed to make me jealous? It's a good thing you haven't seriously set your cap at me, because that wouldn't make me jealous. In fact, nothing would. I'm not the jealous kind.'

'I know that, and you know that, but my mother doesn't know it. And besides, even if she did, it wouldn't change anything. Not only am I meant to talk to other gentlemen to make you jealous, I'm meant to view them as something to fall back on if you don't come up to scratch!'

'Your mother doesn't do things by halves,' he said with a laugh. 'In that case I'll have to let you go for a while. Don't worry, I'll glower and glare as though I'm suitably jealous if your mother glances my way. But you must make sure you let me take you into supper. My mother made me promise I would.'

'In that case, I'd be delighted.'

Just then Alex walked in.

'Do you know him?' asked Mr Ullcaster, turning to look at Alex as he followed Lizzie's eyes.

'Yes,' Lizzie said.

'Then if you're going to make me jealous perhaps you should make a start by going over and talking to him.'

'To Alex? How would that make you jealous?' asked Lizzie in astonishment.

'Just look at him,' said Mr Ullcaster. 'Any man would be jealous if the woman he wanted to marry left his side in order to talk to such a wild rake.'

Goodness, thought Lizzie, Raymond thinks Alex really is a rake. The girls and I have done our job very well.

And Alex has done his job well, she thought, seeing how he'd slipped into the role. It was really no wonder Raymond was deceived. Lounging negligently against a pillar with a mocking look on his face, Alex was full of arrogant charm. His hair, now spilling over his collar, was long and wild. His figure was hard and firm. His clothes, so tight they seemed moulded to him, had just the right mixture of fashion and devil-may-care about them. His chin, instead of being clean shaven, was covered with a dark shadow. And his expression was a perfect combination of arrogance and contempt.

Yes, Alex had done his job well.

A little too well, she couldn't help thinking with a strange shiver.

She felt a touch of loneliness as she realized that, if Alex decided to stay as a rake, she would lose her best friend.

Chapter Twenty-Eight

So Wrexham's here, thought Sophy nervously as the musicians finished playing. Well, it's now or never. If I'm going to speak to him I have to do it before I lose my nerve.

He was talking to Mrs Frobisher, a notorious widow. As a rule, Mrs Frobisher kept men dangling on a string. But try as she might, she wasn't able to keep Lord Wrexham dangling. He was already looking bored.

In another minute he's going to make her a mocking bow and walk off, thought Sophy. Which is exactly what he did.

She took a deep breath and followed him. She'd made up her mind to talk to him and was determined not to change it. She followed him out into the hall.

'Wrexham,' she said.

He turned round at the sound of her voice and gave her a strange look. If she hadn't known better she'd have thought it was a look of disappointment. But that was impossible. He had nothing to be disappointed about.

'Let me give you a word of advice,' he said. 'Rakes aren't worth the effort. I like you, Sophy, but don't waste your time falling in love with me. I told you before I was a drunkard and a gambler and — '

'I've no intention of falling in love with you.'

'No?' His smile was so wicked it made her go weak at the knees.

Courage, she told herself.

'No. And as for the drinking and gambling, that's what I want to talk to you about.'

He threw her a cynical look. Then reaching out he stroked her face, sending shivers up and down her spine.

She took a step back. 'It's no good playing those games with me. I know how they work.'

'You do?'

'Of course. Haven't I spent the last few weeks teaching Alex how to be a rake?'

'But he had to be taught,' said Wrexham softly. 'He wasn't born that way.'

She gathered her wits, which was admittedly difficult with Wrexham standing so near, and persevered.

'What I want to know is this. If being a gambler and a drunkard gets you the wrong kind of attention, then why do you go on doing it? Gambling and drinking, I mean?'

He laughed, showing a flash of even white teeth. 'My dear Miss Lyndhurst, are you trying to save me?'

'No.' she shook her head. 'That would be impossible. If you want saving you'll have to do it yourself. I just want to know why you go on doing it, that's all.'

He looked at her curiously. 'Very well. I'll tell you. I do it because my estate is mortgaged.'

'Are you surprised?' she asked.

'Not because of my dissolute ways,' he said. 'It was mortgaged when I inherited it. I wanted to clear the mortgage but had no way of doing it. And then I had some luck at cards. I thought if I could win enough money, I could pay off the mortgage and rebuild my ancestral home. So I gave it a try. At first it went well. But then I started losing. I lost all I'd won, and then went on losing more, so that I was worse off than when I'd started. So then I started drinking to forget about the gambling. And then a strange thing happened. Society women started flirting with me. It was a heady experience. I found I could have any woman I wanted, and it helped me to forget, at least for a while. And now . . . now there is no way out.'

'But can't you find another way to pay off the mortgage?' asked Sophy practically. 'What about selling some of your land, and then using the money you get to pay off the mortgage on the rest of it.'

'No,' he said vehemently. 'I inherited five thousand acres and I mean to pass on five thousand acres.'

'With a huge mortgage and a house that's falling down. It's not much to pass on, in my opinion. It seems more like a burden than a bequest. But if you sell some of the land and then pay off the mortgage you'd pass on something worth having. Not as much, perhaps, but unencumbered. And then your sons won't have to fall into the trap you've fallen into, of gambling to try and raise the money for the mortgage, and instead losing more and getting deeper into debt.'

For a moment she thought he liked the idea. But then he shook his head and said, 'You're a sweet girl, Sophy, but it's too late for me. We each of us go to the devil in our own way, and I must go to him in mine.'

'Only if you choose to do so. But I can see you are determined so I will bid you goodnight.'

She went back into the drawing-room and to her surprise she found that she was shaking. It wasn't surprising. What had she been thinking of, telling Lord Wrexham what to do? She must have taken leave of her senses.

Still, it was over now. She wouldn't attempt to do anything so foolish again.

As she began to recover her composure she noticed that Mrs Frobisher was glowering at her. The widow had obviously seen her going out into the hall and drawn her own conclusions.

After glowering for a few minutes more, Mrs Frobisher left her own clique and joined Sophy at the side of the room.

'A friendly word of warning,' she said. 'I should stay away from Lord Wrexham if I were you. He has a scandalous reputation, and is too strong a meat for little girls.'

'I have no intention of going near him ever again,' remarked Sophy serenely. 'You are welcome to him. For you, at least, are not a little girl.'

And having delivered this set-down she accepted the Honourable Mr Travis's arm and went into supper.

Chapter Twenty-Nine

Alex, meanwhile, was enjoying himself. As soon as he swaggered into the room heads turned, and Arabella's was one of them. He deliberately took no notice of her. To begin with, she looked away again and tried to pretend she wasn't interested. But after a short time wrestling with herself she walked over to him, fluttering her eyelashes and playing with her fan.

'What a surprise seeing you here tonight,' she said.

He raised his eyebrows and favoured her with a scornful smile.

She flushed, and made as if to walk away. But a minute later she turned back.

'I didn't know you liked music,' she said.

Again, he didn't reply. Instead, he let his mocking glance trail over her from head to foot, stopping at strategic points along the way.

'I am very fond of it myself,' she said.

'Really?' He permitted himself the one word, but loaded it with derisory amusement.

Arabella flushed. 'Yes. Really.'

His look spoke volumes: that she wasn't interested in the music, she was interested in him. It was all very gratifying. And he was pleased there were musicians there, because as soon as they began to play he knew what he was going to do.

The guests started to take their places on the chairs in front of the music stands whilst the musicians tuned their instruments.

'Would you . . . ' Arabella swallowed, as though she was finding it difficult to get her words out. 'Would you like to sit with me.'

He didn't reply. Instead, he pulled her into an alcove and whispered wickedly, 'Meet me in the conservatory in five minutes.' Then without a backward glance he swaggered into the conservatory. Exotic plants combined with elegant furniture to create a sumptuous atmosphere, just right for sweeping Arabella off her feet.

He moved one or two plants to make more room in the centre of the conservatory. He didn't want to spoil everything by tripping over a potted plant in the middle of the waltz. And then he lounged negligently behind the door, waiting for Arabella to arrive.

And of course she did. Funny to think how quickly he'd come to take it for granted. A few weeks ago, if Arabella had agreed to meet him in the conservatory he would have been overjoyed. But now he had come to expect it. But one thing troubled him. When would he revert to his true self and stop pretending to be a rake? After he asked her to marry him? Or should he do it when he was about to propose perhaps? Or wait until they were already married? Should he just tell her straight out: "Arabella, I'm not a rake?" Or should he simply go back to being his ordinary self, perhaps going down to breakfast on the morning after their wedding in his dressing gown, with his hair cut short and his chin neatly shaved.

He started to get a cold feeling in the pit of his stomach. It had all seemed like such a good idea at the time, but if Arabella agreed to marry a rake, wouldn't she expect to marry a rake? Wouldn't she be disappointed if she found herself married to someone who wasn't a rake? And wouldn't she be justified in feeling disappointed?

It had never seemed possible that he would come so far. Oh, in his dreams yes, but always, at the back of his mind, had been the belief that he couldn't do it, that he would never have women falling at his feet, so the idea of what would happen when they found out what he was really like hadn't bothered him.

He was still pondering the problem when the door opened and all thoughts of everything else were driven out of his mind by the sight of Arabella, looking more breathtakingly beautiful than he had ever seen her. He knew exactly what to do. He'd been planning it for days. He materialised from out of the shadows behind the door and caught her round the waist, dragging her towards him and crushing her in a tight embrace. Then he looked down at her with a smouldering look.

Her eyelids drooped. She almost swooned in his arms, and she turned up her face for his kiss.

But he'd learnt his lesson well. Rakes never did what women wanted, or expected, them to do. That was part of their appeal. They always did something else. So instead of kissing her, he took her chin in his hands, looked at her intently, and said, 'You have a smut on your face.'

Seeing her look of embarrassed confusion he let her go, smiling mockingly at her distress. As he did so, he wondered why he didn't mind behaving in this way any more, when to begin with he'd thought it was cruel to treat women so badly. Maybe he was becoming a real rake, he thought, in which case he need never disillusion Arabella. Maybe he could spend the rest of his life embarrassing her and confusing her. She seemed to like it.

The thought that Arabella, although extremely beautiful, was not very clever slid through his mind.

Lizzie was clever. She wouldn't like it if he made her feel foolish all the time, that much was certain. Besides, if he told her she'd got a smut on her face she wouldn't feel foolish. She'd simply look in the mirror, and if there was one she'd get rid of it, and if there wasn't . . . well, then she'd put him down in no uncertain terms. But then Lizzie wasn't like other women.

Meanwhile Arabella was blushing prettily. She was trying to look at herself discreetly in the window and rubbing at her face with her handkerchief.

He could spare her the trouble by telling her there was nothing there, but he had a feeling she wouldn't like him if he was kind to her so he changed his mind and left her to cope as best she could.

'Has . . . has it gone?' she asked hesitantly. She looked at him beseechingly.

He decided to put her out of her misery. 'Yes, it's gone.'

She gave a sigh of relief. As she did so her white bosom rose and fell in the most alluring way, but it didn't have its usual effect. Though still enticing, it simple made him think. Oh, Arabella! Why do you have to be so beautiful, and yet at the same time such a ninny?

This was the moment he should pull her into his arms and dance with her, but somehow he couldn't bring himself to do it. If he went through with his plan he would propose to her, but what then? He would either have to spend the rest of his life pretending to be someone else, or tell the truth and look a fool. And for what? For the dubious pleasure of spending the rest of his life with a woman who, though beautiful, was a nincompoop.

The picture faded and another one took its place. He found that, when he looked ahead to the rest of his life, he didn't see Arabella there. Instead, at the centre of every picture, was Lizzie.

Chapter Thirty

Lizzie was in low spirits. Try as she might, she couldn't keep her mind on what Mr Ullcaster was saying. All she could think about was Alex. Because not only would she lose her dearest friend when he married Arabella, she would lose . . . And in a blinding flash it hit her. She would lose the man she loved.

It had been growing on her gradually over the last few weeks and now she wondered why she had never seen it before. She had always assumed she would marry Alex, but she had never known it. When they had talked of teaching their children to swim and fish, it was always Alex she saw there beside her. Even when she and the girls had sworn to be spinsters, she had still thought she would be teaching her children to swim in the river and it had never occurred to her that that would not happen if she remained a spinster. Or if she married someone else.

She had been so blind.

Because she had known Alex all her life she had failed to see how perfect he was for her. It was only when he'd transformed into a rake that she'd seen him with different eyes.

And it wasn't just her eyes that felt differently about him, it was the rest of her, too. When he had swept her into his arms she had felt all tingly, not because she was ill but because she was falling in love.

But now Alex was going to propose to Arabella.

'No!' she shouted.

'Eh?' asked Mr Ullcaster, startled.

'That is, I have to go,' she said hastily.

'Go where?'

But it was too late, Lizzie had already gone.

She hurried round the room, looking for Alex, but he wasn't there.

He's in the conservatory, she thought.

She ran through the guests and came, breathless, to the conservatory. And there was Alex, moving purposefully towards Arabella, who was standing with lips pursed and eyes closed, ready for his kiss.

A wave of despair washed over her.

'Why, Lizzie, is something wrong? You look dreadful. I saw you running off and came to find you. I wondered if Mr Ullcaster had said or done something to upset you.'

It was her mother.

Lizzie turned towards her with such misery on her face that her mother recoiled, then taking in the scene in the conservatory her mother said, 'Ah! I see. Come away, my dear, there's nothing you can do. We will say you have a headache. I will take you home.'

Chapter Thirty-One

'Lord Wrexham!' It was the morning after the soirée. Sophy's mother gasped in astonishment as she looked at the card that had been sent in to her. Then, gathering her wits she turned to the butler and asked, 'Is this a hoax?'

'I'm afraid not,' he said. His voice was sepulchral. 'There can be no mistaking the Wrexhams. It is indeed Lord Wrexham who is waiting below.'

Sophy's mother looked at the card again. She shook her head. 'But what can it mean?'

Sophy felt a blush spring to her cheeks. Lord Wrexham was paying her a visit? What was he thinking of?

Her mother, still puzzling over the meaning of the unexpected card, cast her an astonished glance. But seeing Sophy blush she bit back the repulsing words that were hovering on her lips.

'Oh, well, he may be a rake,' Mrs Lyndhurst said calmly, 'but his family are out of the top drawer. And sooner or later, even in a rake, blood will out. I was at school with his aunt and she was a very fine woman. We may as well see what he wants.' She turned to the butler. 'Show him in.'

The butler left, and a minute later Lord Wrexham walked into the room. He was looking, as always, very handsome, but he spoke to Mrs Lyndhurst with great civility. 'It is good of you to receive me.'

'Not at all.' Mrs Lyndhurst, now she had

recovered from her shock, was poise personified.

The same, unfortunately, could not be said for Sophy, who was feeling distinctly uncomfortable.

'Won't you take a seat?' asked Mrs Lyndhurst.

'Thank you.' He waited for the ladies to sit down and then sat down himself. 'My aunt asked me to remember her to you,' he said, to Sophy's mother, as calmly as though he'd been an eligible gentleman instead of a notorious rake. 'I don't know if you remember her, but — '

'Of course I do,' said Sophy's mother. 'Georgiana and I used to be good friends. We were at the seminary together. I haven't seen her for years, though, not since she moved to Derbyshire on her marriage. And unfortunately she and her husband never come to London.'

'No. My uncle's health has been poor. But they are thinking of it this Season,' said Lord Wrexham, speaking to Sophy's mother but for the most part looking at Sophy. 'She very much hopes to renew your acquaintance.'

'That would be delightful,' said Mrs Lyndhurst. 'We can catch up on old times.' She paused, then said. 'May I offer you some refreshment? A brandy, perhaps?'

'Some tea would be welcome,' he said.

'Tea?' Mrs Lyndhurst was taken aback. But then, recovering herself, she rang the bell to order some tea.

Sophy, meanwhile, didn't know what to think. What was Lord Wrexham doing there? And why was he behaving in such a gentlemanlike manner, so unlike his usual rakish self? It was all very strange.

The conversation petered out.

Mrs Lyndhurst was desperately trying to think of something to say, but couldn't think what to say to someone like Wrexham.

Lord Wrexham was sitting there as politely as possible.

Sophy was wondering what was going on.

A part of her thought Lord Wrexham must have come to see her, but another part of her thought that it was impossible. Why would he come to see her when he had only spoken to her twice in her life, and they had argued the last time they had spoken?

Had he done it to spite her, she wondered, and to make her uncomfortable for having dared stand up to him? It was certainly working if that was the case, because he was making her uncomfortable.

She wished the servants would hurry up and return with the tea.

'Have you been in town long?' asked Mrs Lyndhurst, at last thinking of something to say.

'A few weeks,' he said politely.

And really, why was he being so polite? thought Sophy. It wasn't like him at all.

'Will you be staying for the Season?'

'I might,' he said. He turned and looked at Sophy. 'It depends.'

Neither Sophy nor her mother were brave enough to ask him what it depended on, and they lapsed back into silence until the tea came in.

'Miss Lyndhurst,' said Lord Wrexham when they had finished their tea. 'It's a beautiful day. May I prevail upon you to take the air with me? My carriage is outside.'

Sophy felt her heart beat faster. Take the air with Lord Wrexham? Her reputation would be ruined.

But to her astonishment her mother seemed to think otherwise.

'What a charming idea,' Mrs Lyndhurst said. 'I'm sure Sophy would enjoy that. Betsy will go with you, my dear,' she said, turning to Sophy, Betsy being Sophy's maid. 'Run upstairs and put on your coat and bonnet.'

Sophy couldn't take it in. Her mother was not only allowing, but encouraging, her to go out for a drive with Lord Wrexham. But then, she realized, Lord Wrexham, for all his reputation, was an earl, and the woman who married him would be a countess.

Still, in general, her mother wasn't impressed with titles, and she was finding it hard to believe her mother would encourage such a liaison. Unless her mother believed what she had said when Lord Wrexham's card had been sent in, that blood would always out, and that Lord Wrexham might be a good man underneath, after all.

Whatever her mother's motives, however, she could not refuse to go, and besides, she did not want to. She was intrigued by Lord Wrexham's visit, and wanted to know what lay behind it.

She was glad, even so, that her mother had decided to send Betsy with her. The redoubtable maid had arms like rolling pins and it would be a brave man who would try and take advantage of one of Betsy's charges. And what's more Society knew it. If she was with Betsy she would be safe from Lord Wrexham - although she found that, strangely enough, she wasn't afraid of him - but more importantly she would be safe from any slurs on her character.

Five minutes later Wrexham handed Sophy into his carriage. Then he handed Betsy in after her.

Sophy sat in the front of the carriage, next to Lord Wrexham, and Betsy sat behind them.

'Don't worry, Miss Lyndhurst,' he said as he guided the carriage out into the flow of brewer's carts and other equipages that were thronging the London streets. 'I'm not intending to abduct you.'

'I never thought you were,' she remarked.

'No? You seem to be gripping your seat extremely tightly for someone doing no more than taking a carriage ride.'

Sophy glanced down at her knuckles, which were indeed white, but her tension had nothing to do with fear and everything to do with the strange sensations his close proximity was arousing. She could not, however, admit that to Wrexham.

'The road is full of potholes,' she said. 'I am concerned to keep my seat.'

He smiled, not mockingly but teasingly. She did her best to ignore it, but it wasn't easy as it made her heart do somersaults.

'Why did you call on me?' she asked, to show him that she was not nonplussed.

'Isn't it obvious? I wanted to see you.'

'But that is what I can't understand. We parted on bad terms.'

'You were surprised then, when my card was brought in.'

'I was. And my mother nearly had an apoplexy!' she said, recalling her mother's astonishment.

He laughed. 'It will take more than my card to give your mother an apoplexy. And besides, once she had recovered from her shock, she was pleased to see me. She got on well with my aunt and she knows that, whatever my reputation, I'm an eligible bachelor with a title and a large estate. I will always be welcome to sensible mothers with daughters to get off their hands, no matter how surprised they might be when they first receive my card.'

'Your estate is mortgaged to the hilt,' Sophy reminded him, not wanting to encourage him in his arrogance. 'Mother might think you're an eligible bachelor, but to my way of thinking no man can be really eligible if he is heavily in debt.'

'Which is what I have come to talk to you about.' He turned the carriage into the park and, once the horses were stepping lightly along the carriageway, he said, 'I've taken your advice, you see. I am looking for a buyer for my outlying fields, so that I can pay off the mortgage on the rest of my country estate.'

'Goodness.' Sophy's eyes opened wide in surprise. Wrexham was paying off his mortgage? And in a way she herself had suggested. It was all very strange. And yet at the same time she had to admit that it was gratifying. 'I thought it was too late for you.'

'Maybe it isn't,' he said musingly. 'Mind you, that doesn't solve all my problems. First of all I have to find a buyer, then I have to put my estate back in some kind of order. And after that I have to solve the problem of my town house. Like the rest of my inheritance, it was heavily mortgaged when I came into it, and I've decided to sell it.'

'But surely your house is in Mayfair?' asked Sophy.

'What difference does that make? A mortgage is a mortgage, wherever the house might be.'

'But there are other ways of getting rid of it if the house has a good address. There are plenty of people who want to rent a house in town for the Season, and Mayfair is in the most sought after part of town. It appeals to the newly rich as well as the established families. The wealthy mill owners love to show off their new-found status by renting premier houses, and yours must be one of the best. Added to that is the fact that you are an earl. Any mother with an unmarried daughter is going to want to rent your house for the Season, rather than someone else's, because she will hope you'll see her daughter and fall in love with her.'

Wrexham was surprised. 'I'm hardly likely to do that.'

'You know that, but they don't. And besides, a mother with an unmarried daughter is an eternal optimist. She isn't interested in what's likely to happen, she's interested in what might.'

'It's a good idea,' he said, turning the carriage into another carriageway. 'But it won't work. Mayfair might be a good location but the house is run down and no one wants it.'

'You can't be sure.'

'Yes. I can. I've tried to let it out before and there were no takers.'

'How run down is run down?' asked Sophy, not to be deterred.

'The curtains are moth-eaten and the furniture is battered,' he said. 'The carpets are dusty and the mirrors are chipped.'

'Is all the furniture shabby, or just some of it?'

'I haven't examined every piece — '

'Then perhaps you should. If there is enough good furniture you can use it to furnish the main rooms and put all the battered furniture in the attic,' she explained. 'Then with a few new curtains to brighten up the place — '

'You seem to forget my means are straitened,' he said. 'I haven't any money for new curtains.'

'Then use some of the money you make by selling your land. It's only for a short while. Once the house in Mayfair's been let it will bring in more money and then you can pay off the mortgage on the town house, and use any extra to help pay off the mortgage on your country estate as well.'

He looked thoughtful. 'It might work. Will you help me to choose the new curtains and arrange the furniture?'

She thought about it. A part of her felt it would be unwise to spend too much time with Lord Wrexham, but a part of her found the idea appealing. 'Very well. And if the house is as dusty as you say, I can chivvy the servants. Without a mistress they grow lazy, and that's when the carpets stop getting beaten.' She hesitated. 'You do have servants in your town house?'

'Yes, I do. Not many, but one or two. The house is shut up out of season, but I hire a couple of servants each February to look after the house whilst it is open.'

'Good. Then the sooner we get to work the better. The Season proper is almost upon us and the house has to be ready for then.'

'You're a remarkable woman, Miss Lyndhurst,' he said softly, as he turned the carriage for home.

'Spare me your flattery. You forget, I've had a hand in making a rake, and I'm immune to their ways.'

'This isn't flattery. As I hope one day to prove.'

Chapter Thirty-Two

Lizzie was in the drawing-room, trying to make up her mind what to do. She had been so upset the night before that she had allowed her mother to take her home, but a good night's sleep had shown her how lily-livered she had been and she was determined to go and see Alex and tell him that she loved him.

But just as she was about to put on her bonnet there came a rap at the door and a minute later Alex was shown in.

'Alex! I wasn't expecting you!' she said in delight.

'You thought I'd be still in bed? Not on a lovely day like this. Shall we take a walk in the park?'

'A good idea. I never could bear being cooped up inside on a day like this.'

She put on her cloak and bonnet and, together with Miss Withershanks, they set out.

'You seemed to be getting on very well with Arabella last night,' said Lizzie as they made their way to Hyde Park, which was conveniently close at hand. 'But Alex, the thing is . . . '

There was a wistfulness in her voice that made Alex's heart beat faster. He knew he loved Lizzie but until that moment he hadn't been sure of her feelings for him. Oh, there were times when he thought she had started to think differently about him: the moment when he swept her into his arms in Kent was one of them. But at the time he had been so absorbed with Arabella that he hadn't really noticed.

But now it was different. He could feel her trembling a little and her hand, which was placed on his arm, was quivering. His heart swelled with joy.

'Yes, I was. But do you know, Lizzie, once I'd got her under my spell, I realised I didn't want her any more. I realised that, if I had to pretend to be something I'm not in order to win a woman, then the woman isn't worth the winning. The woman I really want –'

'Yes?' she asked breathlessly.

'The woman I really want is one who knows me inside and out, and loves me anyway. I think I'm right, aren't I, Lizzie. You do love me?'

'Oh, yes, Alex, I do. When I saw you in the conservatory with Arabella last night, that's when I was sure. I wanted to burst in and say, "No, you can't marry Arabella, you have to marry me."'

'You did?' he asked in surprise.

'Yes, I did. I made it as far as the door, but when I saw her turning up her face for your kiss and I saw you striding towards her, I was overcome with misery. At that moment Mama came up and understood everything, so she said she would take me home.'

'Ah, so that's why I couldn't find you when I left the conservatory.'

'What do you mean?'

'I never got as far as kissing Arabella because I knew I was in love with you. I tried to find you but you had already left.'

'And why did you want to find me?' she asked.

'Why, to ask you to marry me, of course. Will, you, Lizzie?'

'Yes, I will!'

He turned towards her, and to the scandal of Miss Withershanks he kissed her.

They emerged from their embrace to hear a familiar voice. It was Jane.

'At last!'

'We've been wondering when you would see it,' said James, who was with her.

'You don't mind?'

'No, of course not, how could we mind. We are both delighted for you.'

'But it means the end of the spinsterhood.'

'As to that, it was doomed anyway,' said Jane. 'James and I are going to be married.'

'Oh, Jane, I thought you might! That's wonderful,' said Lizzie.

Alex and James shook hands.

'Now it just leaves Sophy,' said Jane. 'Oh dear, I hope she won't be too upset.'

'I think she will survive,' said James with a twinkle in his eye.

They followed his gaze and saw Sophy and Wrexham driving towards them.

'Wrexham?' said Lizzie. 'Oh dear, are you sure? He has a terrible reputation.'

'But he is one rake who is determined to mend his ways,' said James. 'Sophy's mama knows Wrexham's aunt, and my mother knows her, too. In fact, my mother knew Wrexham as a little boy. She always felt there was good in him. It just took Sophy to bring it out.'

Wrexham's carriage drew level with them and they were soon sharing their news. Sophy was delighted to know that her friends were betrothed, and from the look of genuine pleasure on Wrexham's face it was clear he was no longer opposed to matrimony either.

'If I don't miss my guess, a proposal from Wrexham will soon be on its way,' said Alex, as they all finally parted: James was taking Jane home, Wrexham was driving Sophy home and Alex was taking Lizzie home.

'I think so, too. What would you say to a joint wedding?'

'All three of us to marry at once? The idea has a certain appeal, but no, Lizzie, I don't think I can wait that long.'

'It's probably a good thing. If we all married at once then I would miss my chance to be a bridal attendant,' said Lizzie. 'This way we have three weddings to look forward to instead of one. But the wedding I'm looking forward to the most is ours.'

'Shall I marry in my rake's clothes, do you think?'

'No. They're very nice, and you look absolutely wonderful in them,' said Lizzie with a happy smile. 'But I like you better just as you are.'

Cousin Winifred

Winifred Stokes approached the drive of 1 Hill Lane hesitantly because she didn't like what she was about to do. Her pride forbade it, and throughout her life, her pride had been her staunchest ally. It had stood by her when her parents had died. It had enabled her to reject charity, and it had encouraged her to apply for a position as a governess. It had bolstered her faltering courage when she had learnt that governesses needed to be able to play two instruments and speak half a dozen languages, and told her that a nursery governess needed none of these abilities. And since a nursery governess was all she was fit for, a nursery governess she would be.

She encouraged herself with thoughts of a bright future, in which she would bring joy to the hearts of babes who would lisp out their love for her in between their alphabet.

Unfortunately, Master Charlemagne Abattoir, by some strange quirk of fate, did not share her vision of their future together, for he had his own. He enjoyed kicking her on the shins when he was not eating, and throwing his food at her when he was.

His darling Mama – a name bestowed on that lady by herself – could not understand how Winifred could be so wicked as to encourage her angel to make sport with his food, and thought there must be something wrong with Miss Stokes. This suspicion was confirmed by Master Charlemagne's behaviour, for if Miss Stokes did not merit a kick in the shins then why, pray, would Master Charlemagne administer one?

Appalled by Winifred's obscure yet certain criminal tendencies, Mrs Abattoir sent her packing, for she could not sleep at night thinking of her dear Charlemagne being contaminated by That Woman.

That Woman soon found another position, but Miss Esmerelda Dimple showed no more inclination to love and admire Winifred than Master Charlemagne had done. Instead, she showed the same desire to admonish Winifred, albeit by a nip on the arms instead of a kick on the shins.

Miss Dimple's dear Mama had no hesitation in dismissing the odious Miss Stokes, who had surely encouraged Esmerelda to remove her ribbons and, with them, try to strangle the cat. And Winifred was again left penniless and positionless.

Spare lodgings turned into meagre lodgings. Meagre lodgings turned into grim lodgings. Then grim lodgings turned into no lodgings.

Winifred's pride made an attempt to rally, but a night on the streets – despite the invigorating fresh air and the beauty of the stars – caused her pride to wilt. Indeed, her pride found that it was in need of some pride of its own, to bolster it up, and so it temporarily decamped to look for some.

Taking advantage of its absence, Winifred took the step she knew she must take. She proposed to throw herself on the mercy of her relatives before her pride returned to forbid it.

Her relatives consisted of some distant cousins several times removed who lived at Hill Lane, Little Snodham. Despite her belief that they would jeer at her – deservedly – and refuse her petition –

understandably – she hoped against hope that they might have some nursery-aged children who needed a governess, and who would tolerate her inadequacies on account of being related.

And so it was that she found herself walking up to the front door, where she hesitated again before lifting the knocker and letting it fall.

There was a pause. Nothing happened.

Winifred was tempted to turn and slink away. But *carpe deum* her mother had always said, and if ever a day needed seizing it was surely this one. So she lifted the knocker and let it fall again.

Still there was no answer.

Half relieved and half downcast, she was about to retreat, when she heard the sound of voices coming from the garden behind the house. It sounded as if there was some sort of party going on.

Fearing to intrude, yet fearing to leave because she knew that another night in the bracing fresh air beckoned, Winifred gravitated towards the sound of human voices and human laughter. For once, it was not directed towards her, and it had a pleasant, ringing sound instead of a jeering, braying noise.

As she rounded the corner, nervously exposing herself to view, two pairs of eyes turned towards her and the laughter stopped.

'I'm so sorry, I did not mean to interrupt,' she said, whilst her knees knocked and her teeth chattered and her tattered wings of hope stretched tentatively beside her. 'But I am a relation, a cousin of sorts. My name is Winifred —'

'It's Winifred! Cousin Winifred!' exclaimed the man.

And without further ado, he sprang out of his seat and wrapped his arms around her and planted a big kiss on her cheek.

'Oh, I'm not sure . . . that is to say, we are cousins, but even so . . . ' said Winifred, flustered.

'Everyone, it's Cousin Winifred!' called the man.

The other person present, a cheerful looking woman, came forward, saying, 'Winifred, there you are!' quite as though she were the most welcome person in the world.

'I hope you got my letter,' she said, quite overcome by so much love and affection, for in the previous two minutes she had known more of those delightful commodities than she had ever known in her life before.

'Letter? What letter?' said the man, who introduced himself as Cousin Alf. 'Don't think we got no letter, did we, Pol?'

The woman addressed as Pol said, 'No, no letter. Makes it a surprise. I love surprises. It's better this way.'

'I don't mean to intrude . . . ' said Winifred.

They looked at her, mouths agape, and she realised that the concept of intruding was entirely unknown to these lucky, happy people.

Around the corner of the house came a younger man, a man so radiantly handsome, with bronzed skin, blue eyes and brown hair, that Winifred's poor heart - having spent its life in solitary confinement - did a sprightly somersault, followed by a jig.

'Harry! Just in time,' said Cousin Alf.

'Just in time for what?' asked the man.

Without waiting for a reply, he picked Pol up and threw her gaily over his shoulder, making her squeal with delight. Then he spun her round before dropping her to the ground again and giving her an enormous bear hug before letting her go; the whole thing giving great satisfaction to both.

'To meet Cousin Winifred,' said Alf with a laugh.

'So that's who it is,' said Harry. 'Have a bite, Winifred?' he asked, and waved his arm behind him. Winifred saw that a table loaded with good things in the direction of his wave.

'Oh! So kind! But no, not possibly, I couldn't.'

Winifred's stomach had been well brought up and it knew it must refuse refreshment, no matter how starving it might be. It had never quite worked out why it should say no to sustenance when it was growling with hunger, but being well schooled by Winifred's poor, beleaguered conscience, it had meekly accepted the fact.

'Why not?' asked Alf.

'Yes, why not?' asked Pol.

'Oh, well,' said Winifred, wondering as much as they did, *Why not?* 'I must thing of my figure,' she said vaguely.

They looked at her, mouths agape.

'Think of your figure?' asked Harry.

Before Winifred had time to reply, round the corner came another woman, a woman of noble – nay, generous – proportions; a roly poly of a woman with a sparkling smile, a bosom like a bolster and hips like the rolling swell of the sea. She was clad in a scarlet, clinging gown, and she shook all over with laughter like a raspberry jelly.

The strange thing was, although Winifred had been taught from an early age that anyone not as thin as a lath was a glutton, a weak and despicable person with no self respect or will power, she thought the woman was the most beautiful person she had ever seen. Round rosy cheeks, pearly white teeth and curls of golden hair set off her ample rolls of flesh, turning her into a goddess of fruitfulness and plenty.

'Here, Clementine, Cousin Winifred's watching her figure!' said Alf.

Clementine let out a gale of mirth.

'What do you want to watch your figure for, a slender thing like you?' she asked.

Slender.

The word rang golden in Winifred's ears.

No one had called her slender before. Scraggy, scrawny, a piece of string, yes. Slender, no.

And what a word it was, conjuring up visions of youth and beauty, suppleness and elegance, desirability and worth.

I am slender, thought Winifred happily.

'Here,' said Harry, heaping strawberries in a bowl and ladling them with cream.

'Oh, my goodness!' said Winifred.

As if in a dream she took them and began to eat.

It isn't real, she told herself. *I'll wake up soon, I know I will, but I must stay here as long as I possibly can.*

She scooped up a spoon of strawberries and cream. The flavours danced and swirled on the tip of her tongue.

'So, Winifred, got any nippers?' asked Alf.

'Any — ?' asked Winifred.

'Children, little 'uns,' said Alf.

'Oh, *no*,' said Winifred, shocked. 'I am not married, you see.'

Alf let out a roar of laughter.

'Didn't stop our Clementine,' he said.

Clementine wobbled like a jelly, rocking with mirth.

Oh, goodness, thought Winifred.

She began to form a severe reply, when she remembered it was only a dream.

'Well, there's time yet,' said Alf.

'Time?' gasped Winifred.

This glorious man with his glorious words opened up vistas of possibilities. *Time yet.* But, alas, those vistas quickly dimmed.

'I am afraid not,' she said. 'I am nearly 40, you know.'

'How nearly?' asked Alf.

The question shook her. She had expected a gentlemanly reticence, instead of which he had broken with all convention and Asked A Lady Her Age.

But what did it matter, after all, if it was a dream?

'I am 38 in October,' she said.

'October? Who said anything about October?' asked Alf. 'October might never happen. You're 37.'

She did not know quite how he had done it, but he had reduced her "nearly 40" to "37", thereby sweeping three years off her putative age.

But this marvellous man had not finished with his miraculous mathematics.

'Seems to me, if we're talking in nearlys, you're nearly 35,' he said. 'Leastways, a lot nearer 35 than 40.'

She saw him in a nimbus of light. He had now reduced her age to 35, and done it with such a careless air, that any casual listener might believe him.

'So, got anyone in your sights?' asked Alf.

'Oh, no,' said Winifred, flustered.

'You could do worse than Harry.'

'Harry?' asked Winifred in a failing voice.

Alf thought she could marry *Harry*? She, Winifred Stokes, thin as a drain, unloved, unwanted, unprepossessing; bearer of bruises and battered shins and owner of a grubby skirt and jumper, occasioned by her night under the stars? S*he* could do worse than Harry?

'She might do worse, but she can do better,' said Pol. 'You've only got to look at her to see that she's a lady.'

Better than Harry? thought Winifred in a haze. No one in her life had ever thought she could do better than anything before, not even better than living in an attic in someone else's house and being pinched and kicked by their children. And here was Pol, saying she could do better than Harry; better than spending her life with a bear of a man who had laughing eyes and hugging arms and —

Oh, my goodness! thought Winifred, carried away by the splendid vision of herself walking down the aisle with Harry. *It's true that blood is thicker than water. These people think I am worth something because I am family! How foolish I was to stay away for so long.*

But the delightful vision that beckoned her was swiftly punctured by reality, which had a habit of intruding when it was least wanted and least expected.

Winifred discovered that she was not in fact dreaming, as she had suspected, because if she had been dreaming she would not have allowed the garden gate to open and she would certainly not have allowed a pinched man to enter, exuding an air of sourness that made the flowers wilt in misery.

'Ah, Cousin Winifred,' he said, 'I am your cousin Algernon. I saw you turning into the lane from the upstairs window, and when I then perceived that you had turned left into Hall Lane instead of right into Hill Lane I felt it incumbent upon me to rescue you from such vulgar company and escort you to your relatives. Though if you are so foolish as to lose yourself again, you must not expect me to rescue you. I'm a very busy man and I can't waste my time on silly women who don't know their Hills from their Halls. Well, come along then, the child is waiting. You will not have time to unpack because Master Nero is not accustomed to waiting for his nursery nurse, and he will be very angry if you are late. Although he is only six years old, he is already accustomed to disciplining unruly staff, and you will find yourself sent to bed without any supper if you do not make haste.'

Alf and Harry and Pol and Clementine listened to this speech with mouths agape. Winifred's spine was so heartened by their unspoken support that it found itself turning into the finest steel, instead of wilting – as was its usual custom – like a piece of week-old celery.

'Thank you, Cousin, but I will not be returning with you. If I am to live on cold charity, I would rather live on the cold charity of strangers than the cold charity of relatives.'

'Charity?' said Harry. 'Who's going to give you cold charity? I'd like to see them try. I'll knock their blocks off.'

Winifred thrilled to the core. No one had ever championed her before. In her hour of need she had always remained needy, but glorious Harry was entering the lists on her behalf.

Alf shook his head and sucked in through his teeth.

'Can't do that, Harry. Winifred's not family no more,' he said.

'Alf's right,' said Pol.

'Better make her family then, hadn't I?' said Harry. 'I'm a bit of a rough diamond but how about it, Winifred?'

When Winifred had dreamt of receiving a proposal – as she often had, in her younger and more hopeful days – she had dreamt of a knight on horseback, who would slide off the horse and land on one knee beside her, with his hand over his heart. But Harry's manly proposal was far better than her most extravagant daydream.

'Are you asking me to marry you?' she asked, almost fainting with joy.

'I reckon I am,' said Harry.

Carpe deum. Her mother's words rang in her ears. And so, very firmly *carping* the *deum*, she said,

'I accept.'

Harry's laughing blue eyes danced and his wide mouth smiled. He picked her up and threw her over his shoulder in an excess of high spirits then spun her round and let her drop neatly into his arms before carrying her across the threshold.

Her sense of Propriety was shocked as he then carried her towards the stairs. But Winifred had had enough of Propriety and she sent it round to Cousin Algernon's, where she knew it would be wanted.

As Harry carried her into the bedroom, Winifred prepared to lie back and think of England, as she believed was the custom on such occasions, but she was surprised to find that she never thought of England once.

In the interests of completeness, my fair reader might like to know that Harry and Winifred were married; Alf married an African princess whilst Pol married a sailor and Clementine remained gloriously single. In time, Winifred and Harry's children joined Clementine's own brood and never once thought fit to kick their mother on the shins, pinch her on the arm, or deprive her of her supper, even if she was late with their bath.

And what of Charlemagne Abattoir and Esmerelda Dimple? I hear you ask. These two delightful young people grew up and married each other, living in luxury on the fortunes they had inherited.

Their respective mothers were not so fortunate. They fell on hard times and were forced to move in with the newlyweds. Charlemagne and Esmerelda naturally did not believe in charity and so they made their mothers work for their keep as soon as a family came along.

    Mrs Abattoir and Mrs Dimple now look after Charlemagne and Esmerelda junior. The last time I saw them I applauded their patriotism, for Mrs Abattoir was sporting blue shins whilst Mrs Dimple was displaying red arms. They were in the company of Cousin Algernon, whose pale complexion supplied the white of the Union Jack. I believe his pallor was caused by going without supper for six days out of seven, because he now finds himself obliged to reside with Master Nero, and he is never in time for the young Master Nero's bath.

Printed in Great Britain
by Amazon